SEAN MACKAAY

Lunch Eater

First published by Letter3 Publishing 2023

Copyright © 2023 by Sean Mackaay

This novel is entirely a work of fiction. The names, characters and incidents portrayed in it are the work of the author's imagination. Any resemblance to actual persons, living or dead, events or localities is entirely coincidental.

Sean Mackaay asserts the moral right to be identified as the author of this work.

First edition

ISBN: 978-0-6459602-1-1

This book was professionally typeset on Reedsy.
Find out more at reedsy.com

Contents

For Howard
who escaped

Take a look at these hands
Take a look at these hands
The hand speaks
The hand of a government man
- "Born Under Punches (The Heat Goes On)",
Talking Heads

Chapter 1

No one ever *accidentally* takes your lunch.

How many times have you accidentally opened up the fridge at your job and taken someone else's lunch? Not ever.

It doesn't happen.

Some people would have you believe that this is an accident. They took your triple stack BLT without realising. How were they supposed to know that the honey mustard chicken salad in glassware they have never purchased was yours?

This, of course, is nonsense. No one makes this mistake.

Malicious creatures haunt every workplace. They smile as you walk past them in the corridors. They smile knowing what they have done to you. These creatures that look like you and I wander the halls of your office. They shamble through mine. The taste of your lunch still fresh on their tongue.

There is no common background that makes a person turn Lunch Eater. Nothing that you can point to and say, "Ah yes, of course, they turned into a Lunch Eater."

Chapter 2

Our lords and masters work up on the hill. You've seen them on television. You've read about them in the newspaper. People often think it's the politicians that come up with the policies. Certainly, they are the ones that take it in the neck when it doesn't work out.

In fact, it is us mandarins, who have no exposure to the real world, sitting in our offices, staring out across rivers and dreaming those policies up.

While the politicians may feel the rage of the public, they turn that on to us. No feeling quite like management telling you that the Minister's Office called. Politicians are that rare breed of sociopath that never learnt the childhood lesson of not paying anger forward.

And yet, like an abused spouse, we keep shuffling into the office to be beaten by our lords and masters. Which you could say is what they pay us for. Of course, it does mean that you learn an odd brand of fear that you don't experience outside of the service.

You hang on their every word. Scanning newspapers and talkback radio summaries. Scouring media statements like they are some arcane incantation. In case one of the politicians has said something that has blown up six months of work. Or that will consume the next 2 years of your life. Or that actually affects you as a human being.

Not that you are supposed to be a human being. They drum it into you in university. You are a vessel for the politicians' words to come to life. Like you are a savant channelling words from a higher plane. You are not supposed to be political despite working so close to politics.

Some do it better. I like to consider myself one of them. Sure, when I was in university I was liberal-leaning radical. That's just the way of things. The way of youth. Identity politics and challenging the existing structures.

Of course, there are the servants that never went to university. They're easy to spot. There's a malice to interactions with them. A grudge that they didn't go to university and think everyone looks down on them.

It's a sad fact but generally they don't get much higher than mid-level in the service. It isn't an education thing, though they think that is the case. It's that they never built up a network of connections that they can lean on to get parachuted into whatever plum role they have their eyes on. Claire was one of those. She never could understand why she was looked over for the jobs she actually wanted.

They don't realise that the class warfare extends to those of us that went to university. No one really cares what university you studied at or what your degree is, it's not like you use any of that knowledge in your work. They do care about what school you went to before university. That tells them your pedigree. That tells them your family and the environment you were raised in. That opens doors because you might have built up a network in university but they were born into networks that they leverage to get ahead.

Early on in my tenure as a servant, I realised the best method was to be hollow. The first time you land a policy setting that leads to controversy and fallout, you are harrowed. The media spotlight is on your politician and you are bombarded with requests for briefings and advice and responses to media enquiries. Your days become too long. Charlie appears in the corners of your vision too often. Your body is exhausted but you can't sleep. The old ones, they shake their head and sigh as they walk past you. One of them will finally take you under their wing and tell you that you need to stop caring, that if you realise that none of this matters than you might just survive.

There is no need to feel anything about the levers you are being instructed to pull. A politician stands up and says that no longer shall people of colour be allowed to graduate from universities. Other politicians agree and you're off to the races.

From that point on you need to work out how you're going to make a blatantly racist policy (or piece of legislation, as that happens sometimes) work. Because you can't just put through a bill that bans people of colour from attending university. That would be racist. If something is so blatantly racist, you can expect the judiciary to throw it out (or at least make you jump through hoops to make it work).

Then you and all your policy brethren have to come up with a way of disguising the policy so the outcome still happens but people don't march up the hill with torches and pitchforks. We call it disincentivising. How can you make it so hard that people of colour won't bother with university? How can you place an economic burden on them so hefty that even if some of them get the bold idea to go to university that the success of graduation will cripple them for the rest of their lives?

So you see, to come into the office with a political bent will only lead to you burning out. Sooner or later, one of our masters will want to do something that you can't handle. That makes you snap. You might not stroll through the office with an automatic weapon but you will go… wrong. A wrong that makes your coworkers take notice. That they will talk about in hushed tones. That may even get you facing disciplinary action with HR.

You often find with the older sort t became servants because they believed. They believed that serving the public was a great thing to do. That undertaking the service, despite the fact that people would hate them, despite the fact that no one ever got rich off the service (and those that tried to end up in prison facing corruption charges), that somehow it was so noble.

Perhaps it's something to do with my generation but you look around and you see people your age accepting whatever our masters want from us. And those older just look drained.

Some election cycles you don't even need to read who won, you can just tell by looking at the old liberals and conservatives in the office. The deflated ones tell you which side is ascendant.

Chapter 3

There are 3 types of lunch.

The run out of the office and grab something so you can eat at your desk and prove to your boss that you're busy. Boxed sandwiches. Terrible salads. Starting to turn bad sushi.

The specifically put together for lunch at the office. Can be prepared in bulk if you can keep them fresh enough. Hastily thrown together sandwiches. Perfectly manicured salads. Health kick smoothies.

The leftovers.

In some cultures, those lunches that have been specifically made dominate the market. In India, the dabbawallahs and tiffin wallahs keep office workers fed and create roaring employment opportunities for the deliverers. In Japan, convenience stores provide a good level of bento for those salarymen that don't have the time to sit at a ramen bar.

Here though, it is the run out of the office lunch that keeps people fed. What people return with from their modern day hunting and gathering tells you a lot about their station in life. The boss that gets Japanese every day. The soon-to-be retiree has enough saved to be able to afford to buy a boxed Thai salad from the good Thai place that is around the corner and down that alley.

The leftovers present a tightrope. The best of meals may not keep the day after. Risotto can become too claggy when reheated. Chicken cacciatore needs to be reheated, to make sure the chicken won't kill you, to a point where you waste your entire lunch break waiting for it to cool.

There are days when you will find leftover gnocchi in the fridge. Burnt sage butter, some parmesan and a sprinkle of roasted pumpkin on the top. It reheats well, the cheese springing to life. The pumpkin wilts a little. Sad cubes of orange sitting on top. They taste well enough and are primarily a garnish so you don't mind. The burnt sage butter should be bottled.

It all goes down quite well.

You think of possibly washing the container and putting it back in the fridge but it feels like a bridge too far.

Instead, you wander into one of the conference rooms and place it on a table near the back.

Chapter 4

Before I started my life as a servant, I thought that it would be dynamic and fast-paced. All the smartest people in a room with the best intentions trying to do their best to make the lives of ordinary citizens better.

I imagined we would be pulling levers and pitching ideas and it would be the best job anyone could ever have and why anyone would ever not want to be a servant would be beyond me.

The first year was an eye-opener.

It turns out that when you can't be fired. And you won't profit from what you're doing. And your daily life is dictated by a bunch of privileged man-babies that will come up with insane ideas at the drop of a hat. Well. Most people just don't try very hard.

Which is fine. The public doesn't expect servants to be effective. Some times they expect us to be so ineffectual that they'll start fights with you when you mention what you do for a living.

Which is fine. Turns out when you don't have to worry about your job and you don't have to fight for a pay rise every year, you start worrying less about what the public thinks of you and what you do with your time.

Sure there is some of what I imagined. Mainly though, it's research, modelling, and writing briefing memos. When it isn't the actual work, which most days feels like it doesn't achieve anything and the economy would possibly be better off if we just walked out the door, it's all the bullshit of office life that is magnified because no one can have real consequences for anything.

You start trying to work out when management will be in long meetings so you can time your long lunch with that. You try and work out which quiet rooms are empty and when so you can zone out. You try and gauge the correct balance between inane chatter and the appearance of actually being employed.

One old timer used hthe last 3 years of his job to quietly draft a novel which then went on to be rather successful. I suspect there's at least one guy in the Trade team that is hard at work on a screenplay and may even be taking meetings with studio executives at the office.

I of course never do any of those things. I wouldn't because I don't find I have any hobbies any more. When I try to think back I'm not sure when the last time I did was. Shopping for sex toys and the perfect furnishings for my apartment don't count as a hobbies. Nor does listening to podcasts about politics and foreign affairs. There probably needs to be some passion behind something to call it a hobby and those are just things I do.

For those of us like myself that don't have anything useful we can waste time on, we just look for jobs. The public service is purgatory. We exist as half people with limited interior lives. That happens when you exist in a world where there is no drive or reason to achieve.

Problem is that as a half-person servant, there grows a stench around you. Once upon a time, you'd be lauded for spending most, if not all, of your career in one organisation. That showed loyalty. Then everything broke down and hyper-capitalism became the game we all played and there was no more loyalty because companies were treating us like numbers and nothing more. So most people jump from job to job every few years.

As a servant, particularly as a servant in this agency, that happens a lot less. That stench emanates from you once you've been here too long and you start to become untouchable. Oh sure, you can get interviews for jobs. That's not hard. If day in day out you're writing words to put in politicians mouths or doing the gymnastics required to justify egregious breaches of the public's trust, getting an interview is easy.

No. It's the interview itself that kills you. Not because you say the wrong things or can't demonstrate value. No. Your eyes give you away. There's nothing there. It spooks people. Especially poor interviewers that just want to hire someone. They aren't trained to know what to do when they look in someone's eyes and see nothing there. Humans can sense just as well as dogs when something is off but dogs know it's a threat and they need to sound the alarm, and people have no idea what feels off or what they should do. They might try to shower but it's deeper than that. Some might try and drink too much when they get home that night but the sense of something being wrong with the world will linger into the morning when they wake up hungover and craving a hamburger.

I've been trying for the past decade to get a job somewhere else doing just about anything else. I've been here too long. I have the stench. I'd care more but I just don't have enough in me most days.

Chapter 5

I was going to be a star.

And then I became a public servant. The day I received my results from the public service entrance exam was one of the happiest days of my life. After years of university and toiling away to get the best marks possible, I had been rewarded with top marks on the entrance exam. I was on the golden pathway. In other countries, they would say I had an iron rice bowl. My future was set.

Downsizing, redundancies, fired for performance issues, none of these were issues I had to worry about.

Banks would be happy to give me a mortgage. Women would see me as a stable marriage prospect.

I could have my pick of agencies. I had known where I wanted to end up before even sitting down for the entrance exam. Economic Development. It might not have the glamour of the Foreign Office but who wants to sit across a table from foreigners in a foreign land being laughed at in a foreign language you can't understand?

For me, it was always about being in the engine room. Driving growth. Being measured against key economic indicators. Working towards a new golden age for the nation.

I would be a bureaucrat. A policy wonk. I would dazzle them

with my ideas. My knowledge of the levers to pull to ensure everlasting growth for the economy. Oh, they might call me a mandarin. But I wouldn't care.

People would walk past me on the street and not know they had just walked past a man that ensured they had a job. Money enough in the bank. A house valued at far more than what they had paid. A happy family that they could provide for.

Economic Development was where I was heading and I was going to be a star.

When you score as highly as I did on the entrance exam, the agencies are hungry for you. Happy to put you on the fast track. Promise you the things that you dream they will promise you. Perhaps not to the level that a star athlete is promised by a big college but something akin to the public service version of that.

I would be able to have my pick of areas within the agency as well. I could work on Trade and grow the nation's exports. I could work in the cutting edge technology space and kick start hubs of innovation. What I wanted though was to be in Strategic Policy. The ones that are closest to the levers. It might not involve being out in the field much, and it might be a team that most of the public doesn't even know exists, but if I wanted to make an impact, that's where I wanted to be.

Being on the fast track, there's an expectation that I would quickly move my way up. Maybe I wouldn't be an agency head by the time I was 30 but I would move quickly. Even if it meant that I would bounce from area to area with such speed that years later people would say things like, "I think Mr. Collins used to work with us. I think." Or, "That Brian, you know that runs the agency now, didn't he used to sit next to you?"

Chapter 6

"I don't know."

"What do you mean, 'you don't know'?"

"I knew they were going to be putting up the fees at some point but I didn't think it was now."

"They didn't send anything out to say they were putting it up?"

"No. I mean, maybe and we missed it? Did you see anything? Maybe it went into spam. It shouldn't have, it doesn't normally. But that's what this has to be, nothing else makes sense. She hasn't gotten older and they aren't doing anything new that I can tell."

"Okay, so this is just the new rate."

"I wish that it just cost less, you know."

"So there's that. We need to get the car serviced next week, then what else?"

"You know Ginny, you know at work? The one that was dating that guy, you know, *that* guy. She was saying that when Cranky is old enough, the kids who are growing up now probably won't even learn how to drive. It will be all cars that drive themselves."

"The fuck? What? I was saying something here. You're starting in on self driving cars? You think we'll be able to afford some robot car to chauffeur Cranky around? We're talking money and you're thinking about cars that you don't have to drive?"

"I'm just saying. Like the kids today, they won't even understand what the world was like when they're our age."

"We've got the car service next week. Middle of the month, so that means paying for the phones."

"Plus, Cranky's fees. I was trying to work out the subsidy on it today, I don't get it."

"They make it that way so no one can work out what it is and you never know if you're paying the right thing or they're charging you wrong or whatever. She's 4, so we get what? 60% back but then only if you don't work more than two and a half days but you can do an extra day if you pay extra tax for that day. It's so you can never complain because you never know what amount is right."

"Well, Ginny at work, you know, she was…"

"Is it just you and Ginny there? I never hear you talk about anyone else but Ginny."

"And don't forget that just after that we need to pay for my surgery."

"Fuuuck, yeah, the surgery. I don't think we can do it right now."

"But… I need it. I've been on the waitlist for so long. Last time we… and I ended up having to go to the back of the list. I was lucky that I could get in, to even see the specialist again this time."

"I know. I know, okay. We've got the mortgage coming out a week before that so…"

"What? I can see you want to say something."

"I mean, you don't look bad, do you? It's not all the worst

thing that you can't get the surgery right now, is it?

"You prick! I'm literally shitting myself every other hour and you think it's a good thing that I can't get the surgery I need? Don't try and get cute with me, you were going to say something, say it."

"They're just not sure, at work I mean. They don't know if we're facing some sort of a down turn. There's talk that the government is going to start trying to really hammer the industry. With taxes and I don't know. The higher ups have been starting to have conversations with some of the boys and what I'm hearing isn't great. I'm not saying that I'll be out of my job. I don't think. Just, like Simon was saying that Chris pulled him into the office up on site and was talking around cutting back on his hours. Of course, I'll tell Chris he's a sack of shit that eat donkey dicks but me and Simon came on at the same time and I don't know how it's going to..."

"So we'll make it work. We made it work when Cranky first came along, we'll make it work now."

"How? If they cut me back at work then what do we do? Are you going to stop working? Because we won't be able to afford Cranky going to school plus the mortgage."

"We'll make it work. I'll start shopping at the other place, where we used to get the cheap meat. If they cut back your hours, then maybe you can pick up some work with Brad."

"Fucking Brad..."

"We'll make it work."

"I swear there's a guy sitting somewhere, somewhere up there, and his whole job is to fuck me."

Chapter 7

When you imagine a life, perhaps you imagine something with a family. A wife. Two kids. A house. Some space to call a backyard. Friends over at the weekends for barbecues.

Warmth. Smiles. Laughing.

I don't imagine that anymore. Life has a way of not turning out how we want it to. Not a bad life. Just not what you expected.

A life nearing middle age. Inside an inner city apartment. With chrome taps in the bathroom and two sinks. Two bedrooms. One as a study.

A little box, high above the street below.

No one to share it with.

At some point, I realised I was an odd creature. Someone who could only live by myself.

Not that there hadn't been relationships. I just couldn't sustain them.

Or possibly being myself meant they couldn't sustain.

The lack of ties has meant that my disposable income soars. I can truly play at whim in the hyper capitalist morass that we have created. My furniture is updated every two years. Clean, modern lines. The latest season's colour scheme.

It isn't a bad life but I sometimes wonder if it is a shadow of what I expected.

Not that I want to be out in the suburbs. Suburban living didn't suit me as a child, I doubt it would be my own little slice of heaven now.

I remember my life before I entered the service. Vague on some events.

When I was at university my nights were long and my days full of headaches and too much caffeine. I took full advantage of being away from home.

Now my nights are far shorter. A frozen dinner of some variety. Good nutritional information on the side of the packet. Two episodes of the latest hit show. At the moment it's a South Korean political drama. Next season it will probably be guys pretending to fall in love for a chance to win a weekend away.

Then check the emails to make sure Charlie hasn't sent through anything he deems 'urgent' and needs to be on his desk first thing in the morning. Then bed. A few articles on how government can intervene in market failures to wind down. Then sleep. Or a good attempt at something approximating it.

Repeat.

Perhaps this is the life I have built for myself that finds me on this never ending cyclical path where I walk the same steps every day from the bed to the bathroom to the kitchen to the train station to my desk and back again. It could be that I am some public servant creature that is wearing the same path through a failed life.

Or perhaps this is just all of our lives. Perhaps this is the end goal of late stage capitalism for us servants. For those not fortunate enough, whether through birth or effort, to reap the rewards. The rest of us just reap the whirlwind.

Some evenings, as I expertly chopstick my soba and clean

chicken meal into my mouth, I wonder if accidentally there was a lever that we pulled at some point that lead to this. If maybe, just maybe, this wasn't the inevitable end point. If the industrial revolution didn't need to end up here.

The mechanisation of production, of course, had a massive impact on the human race. No longer was there a need to hunt and gather in the way we had. Now, we could consume. And we did. We aren't post scarcity yet but scarcity isn't something we think about.

Sure, the weight of history could have lead to me being hollowed out and walking a path into the fabric of the earth day in, day out. If Derrick told me that, one morning while we were waiting for Charlie to turn up for our meeting 15 minutes late, I'd probably believe him. I certainly wouldn't argue.

But what if one day Derrick pulled a lever? Or I did. Or a young Charlie before he became the passive aggressive insect man that haunts my dreams. And that lever could have been so innocuous. Years later, that lever dictates that we must follow our paths forever.

Sometimes I think I died years ago.

Chapter 8

The thing about Economic Development is that any business worth its salt doesn't need help. They don't need a hit of taxpayer dollars. They are already a success story. They have an export pipeline that has accounted for possible variations in the market. They know how to talk to government and how to get the best deals.

So why do I get out of bed every morning and come to the office? I could tell you a story about how I'm making a difference. How any of this matters. That last year I provided funding to a dozen companies that have all gone on to become leaders in their markets.

None of that would be true.

What is true is that they pay me well.

They can't fire me.

And the view from the 23rd floor, looking out across the river, is calming.

The guy that sits next me to watches videos on his computer all day. I think he's in a band. All the videos are tutorials on using audio engineering software. I don't ask many questions of him. I'm certainly not going to rat him out for not doing anything.

We work in policy, he could just tell me that this is how he gets into the flow to work through a twisty policy issue. I have no issues with that, we all get to the flow in different ways.

Our team is small. Like an upper middle class family, there's little love or interest in each other's lives. All you need is the broad biographicals and then we can fill the day with chatter about the work.

I like the fit of our team, it's easy to deal with and doesn't ask too much of me. When I had ambition, I wondered what it may be like to manage this team. Enjoying the fit of the team when you're just another servant is one thing. To manage each of them as individuals that you need to be more aware of moment to moment would be something else.

Mostly I know how to navigate all of them in their own unique ways but I know how to do that to make sure I am able to deliver the work. Not so that I can ensure that as a unit we are putting forward whatever it is the leadership is demanding of us at any given point in time.

I've never been convinced that our management achieves that. I've never described our management as easy to deal with and not asking too much of me.

Charlie appears at your shoulder. Soft soled loafers give no hint that he is coming. The sort of appearance that makes you accidentally delete half of the ministerial briefing you were typing at his behest.

An appearance that you know will be the start of another round of micro management. Where performance is judged on whether you can guess the words that he likes that particular part of that particular day for the whatever he has had you working on for the past week.

"I think that we need to be using 'created' rather than 'supported' in the media statement, don't you?" he asks, as though you know all the words that are in the media statement that you drafted two weeks ago and he is only now getting around to reading.

And so, half an hour of my life disappears as we shuffle into a quiet room so that he can passive aggressively tell me every mistake that I have made since I came to Economic Development. The time that I circumvented (the word he uses) his place in the approval chain on the draft of the annual report up the hill. The time I undermined him in front of Geoff about the policy he wanted to put in place to drive job creation, never mind he wanted to put in place a setting that was dripping in supply side thinking which would have lead to a net loss in jobs. That time that I used 'anticipated' rather than 'indicative' in a briefing note and we ended up having to do seven drafts before it finally got out of the agency. As though these performance issues, whether real or imagined, will go on some permanent record somewhere and put my role at the agency in jeopardy.

He exhausts me. But then, so do most things here. A mindless buzzing that occurs around me all day. Achieving nothing and saying we've had a great victory.

This is how it is with Charlie. This is how it has always been.

Even in the beginning when I first came into the agency and I was supposed to be going places.

Often on a Monday morning, the office would resemble something like Speaker's Corner. Workers huddle around desks, taking turns at holding court and spewing forth the weekend life they lived. Children's birthday parties, the weather at the beach, the way the world is around 2am for those of the younger generation.

These impromptu gatherings would often draw Charlie like

a moth to the flame. The chance to connect with his staff was irresistible to him. He had pet names for all his staff. It was clear he had read one or more books on modern management techniques and desperately wanted to incorporate them into the workplace.

He would hover at the edge of the conversation groups.

"I... umm... I went..." but then he would blush in a way that started in his cheeks and accelerated up his receding hairline. No more words would come, a slight stutter and then he would slink off to the next group to try again.

In years gone by we had conversations like he sought now. That was long ago before we found our comfortable rhythm. He'd told me once that his wife sold second hand cars, was quite successful at it. Said that she used the charms she'd used on him to sell the cars. He'd also intimated, one day over a lunch he had invited to me and we had never gone for again, that his family were German and had lived in Germany during World War 2. He seemed remorseful of that fact. The sort of comment that someone drops in conversation that you want to probe further but ultimately the answer is almost going to be that yes, they were Nazis.

Charlie is the sort that thinks that a thousand cuts on you provide him the juice to climb up the ladder.

Not that I have been on any great trajectory or am any closer to being Charlie's boss than I was the day I started. But Charlie has been a mid-level manager since the day I started and with time running out for him you would expect that he'll retire as one.

Perhaps that is enough for him but he sure acts like he wants to go places. The past 2 years he has been more hands-on than I remember him being. I suspect that he knows time is short and he needs to start making his run. At least to the level above so he can have a division under him rather than just a team.

I catch myself sometimes about to ask him what he did before this. If there was anything before this. He could have come in through the exam like me, expecting a fast track like me. I assume that he had a life before this. I wonder if any of us did. Maybe it was just the sense of a memory of a life before this.

A wise man once said that if you sit down at a card table and can't spot the fish within the first two hands that you are the fish. Ready to be devoured by sharks.

In the public service if you can't spot the cowards within a week of starting then it means you are one. If you don't even look for the cowards then it means you're a sociopath.

All of us in the service are one or the other.

I had assumed that Charlie was a sociopath. Most of the mid-level manager types are. Watching him over all these years I came to believe that he was a coward. The way he kowtowed to the division head. The way he would avoid all conflict where possible. The way he would damn you with the faintest of praise when you had the biggest of wins.

Over those years I came to realise that I was a sociopath. Not that I used that for evil. I was just apathetic. Charlie was easy for me to manage because sociopaths never care about cowards.

Chapter 9

Ben had that look on his face like he wanted to talk. It was too early in the morning to properly deal with him. It was too early in the morning for me to properly evade him.

As always he started with chatter about the people we know. People I haven't thought of in years. People that I don't talk to anymore. Sometimes life moves on. Sometimes you come from a relatively small city where just about everyone knows everyone else and when you do your gap year overseas and you meet someone that has met someone from there they ask you if you know them and you do.

Ben was like that but we grew up with almost all the same people but never crossed paths.

Bonding out of the way, he launched his opening salvo, "We're fucked."

There were too many things he could mean. Could have been something a politician said yesterday. There was one time one of our masters stood up and said that our team was responsible for creating 100,000 jobs in a 6 month period. First, we don't create jobs, we support them. Second, the briefing note said 10,000. He forgot his glasses that day.

Could have been something someone in the media was saying about one of our masters. Or the agency head, which is worse than a politician most of the time. Like all servants, even agency heads are supposed to be invisible. Or maybe we have another corruption scandal which will mean we can't move for tripping over auditors for the next year.

There was a Christmas party a couple of years back where Ben and I got quite drunk and sloppy and I don't remember much of the night but Ben has always had a grin on his face whenever someone mentions Christmas since. Perhaps a ghost of the past is coming back to render dues owed.

I did call out Charlie in a meeting the other day when the deputy head was present. Charlie doesn't like it when you embarrass him in front of superiors. He wants to keep climbing the ladder and that happens enough times and you find the ceiling pretty fast.

It could have been anything but Ben's face told me he assumed I had any idea what he was going on about.

"I…" I figured I should probably shoot for something. Fortunately, he quickly jumped in. You can often depend on Ben to respond to grunts and nods and the odd smile calibrated to what you think he wants to see.

"IPCC 6. Man. We're fucked. The world is fucking doomed. There is no way we stop the temperature rising. All those fuck heads up on the hill had years to do something and now they're talking about targets for 30 years out as though a report hasn't just dropped that says we're fucking doomed and it's going to get out of control in the next decade."

Of course. He'd caught me early enough that I hadn't the chance to look over the news. We knew the next International Panel on Climate Change report was dropping soon. I didn't think it was today. But then I didn't think that it was Christmas in 9 weeks time either. My routine was leading to me losing time, or at least not noticing its passage.

"Yeah, I think we all..."

"Look around you, man," I don't know why he always calls me man. Listen to him long enough and you'll notice he spends his days code switching on the fly depending on whether he sees you as an ally, an obstacle, or someone that can strap a rocket to his back and make him an agency head.

"Look around you, man. Look at all of them. They stole the world from us."

From my desk, you can see most of the floor. I took a glance. It was just the same old servants that I see every day. Busily bashing away at keyboards or trying to look like they were.

"Well, I don't know. I don't think you can blame Claire for the world overheating."

"Fuck yes you can. That older generation. All of them. Fuck them. They stole our future. You know I was thinking I'd have kids one day. How the fuck am I supposed to bring kids into a world where they'll go to war over resources. Where they probably will have to live in domes so there is maybe air they can breathe. When I was a kid, I read this book called Z for Zac..."

"Sure but it's not like they did it themselves. You know as well as I do that changes in consumer driven behaviour isn't what's needed. There needs to be a change by industry. Anything else is just passing the buck and laying blame where it doesn't need to be."

"No. You're wrong. I mean the people here on the floor. Claire. Terry. James. The old fuckers who are just holding out for retirement. Where do you think we work? Economic Development. That means growing the economy at all costs. You know what Terry has worked on? Oil and gas was his speciality. He's the one that lead the charge to make sure that coal plants were built so that he could build job hubs. James used to work in Trade. Trade for fucks sake! He used to negotiate massive deals, massive deals, with other nations to take that coal. You can't tell it now because he'll tell you all his stories of travelling the world and he's all cuddly and nice but he used to be a master at growing exports. All of them did this and fucking why? So their friends in industry could get rich, they could maybe get a sweet board seat once they retire from here, and they could be taken for expensive lunches. That was the price they put on the goddamn planet, a fucking degustation menu at a Michelin starred restaurant."

I had to pull him into a quiet room to calm him down. I didn't know what to say. The apocalypse is too big to comprehend. I could get angry like Ben and scream down the floor. Walk right up to Terry and punch him right in the mouth rather than suffer through another hour and a half, derailing conversation where he thinks I'm the other smartest guy in the room.

But my first instinct was to think through what this might do to my day. There was a chance we'd have to kick into action and start developing some sort of proposal. I'd have to work around Ben while developing that otherwise he'd try and send something radical up the line to our masters. Charlie would probably kill it off but he'd want to talk it through, at length, before he did.

Of course, as the business of the day has been raping the earth and profiting since long before I even knew what the service was, there was a good chance that we wouldn't be tasked with anything.

Which would mean that Ben would just stew. There was a chance this is what would send him wrong. He's always had an element of the true believer to him. Sometimes he just cares. Sometimes that means he puts out work that I can only dream of delivering. Sometimes it means that I have to manage him before we're in a room with the deputy head or the head or possibly a politician. The politicians have a tendency to listen to the most passionate voice in the room.

It ends up creating work for me.

Chapter 10

You walk into a meeting room and you see Charlie waiting for you at the table. I knew straight away that it wouldn't be my type of meeting. Not if Charlie was there early.

"So who are we waiting on?"

My go to when I have to spend time alone with Charlie that isn't focused on him 'managing' me. It's the go to public sector way of making conversation when you have nothing to say to one another but you know that the silence should probably be filled with something. I try to bring my laptop with me to most meetings to avoid this idle chatter. Open the lid and read over emails that you have read a dozen times and most people will just try and make themselves look busy as well.

I'd left my laptop plugged in at my desk back on the floor which was a flight of stairs away because some times booking meeting rooms in this place was its own small way of the public sector getting some measure of revenge on us servants.

"The End."

Which was enough to know that this was going to create more work than it was worth.

The End was legendary. Not in a good way. The sort of person that everyone in the agency knew. The sort of person that everyone in the agency would try and avoid if they could.

He'd once been a deputy head back in some early version of the agency. Probably about 3 governments ago. Then he was in Charlie's position. Then he was just a ghost that haunted the agency. He wasn't attached to any area of the agency. He just floated. Ostensibly he was attached to the agency head's office but he didn't have a desk down there and he just made his own work.

He was always threatening to retire but he never did. It was always going to be when there was a change in government. Or after the next election. Or once he put to bed the latest policy change he was championing. All those milestones would come and they would pass and The End kept wandering the halls. Like some spirit that was chained to this particular building. I wondered if the agency moved out of this building if he would just continue turning up here haunting whatever company moved in next.

As a deputy head he'd run into some strife which lead to his slow descent back in to the morass of the middle of the service.

It wasn't that he was corrupt, or so the telling of the story went but it was long before my time. He was just too close to those that were. A couple of managers had run a scam where they influenced other agencies to give out contracts to their friends. It was the sort of scam that probably would have worked too. It wasn't high dollar contracts that got extra scrutiny and it was outside their own agency so it would have been much harder for any auditors to pick up on what was going on.

But the managers were drinkers. One of them was rumoured to be a high functioning alcoholic (the service is full of them). Except sometimes he wasn't so high functioning and he liked to talk.

They ended up serving a prison sentence and the cloud had fallen on those close to them, including The End. He wasn't involved but he was just too close. They couldn't get rid of him, it's not like charges were laid against him. They wanted to keep his brain as well. Canny servants know that keeping a lot of institutional knowledge to themselves makes it hard to replace them. So The End was busted down to a manager role, they said it was due to failures in judgement and they couldn't support someone in a deputy head role that had blind spots like that.

Which meant we were stuck with him. The End talks in a way that Charlie tries to imitate. A lot of pauses in places that don't make you so much want to know what comes next but instead get frustrated by the drawing out of a 10 minute meeting into half an hour.

The problem was that The End was smart. The sort of smart you talk about in percentiles. The sort of smart that meant if you got involved in something he was working on, it was probably going to be high impact and would feature heavily in all sorts of arenas like the media and agency annual reports and political speeches.

A good thing, to be sure, in terms of being able to list on your CV. Less good was the work that would come with it. Politicians don't write their own speeches, you'd have to do that. Annual reports went through too many drafts that you would be expected to go through with a fine tooth comb and comment on. The media would pick things up on the back of media statements and you would have to write those responses as well, plus the talking points for the agency head or the cabinet member when they did interviews with the press.

In some ways, that came with the territory. The End, though, well he dialled that right up. The End came from an age where there were typing pools in the service. Where a lot of white men would have offices they could smoke in, and when they were feeling bored they could walk down to the typing pool, which was staffed by pretty young things, to get their words put on the page, have a flirt, and, if they were bored, partake in some light sexual assault.

The End had never learnt to use a computer, or email, or anything of the things that would be expected someone pulling a salary from taxpayer money in the modern world would be able to do. So he just wandered through the halls, finding young women in whatever team was closest to be his typist for the day. Most hours of the day you could hear him do it because he wasn't quiet about it. Dictating this or that letter. Using the time of some other worker, who probably got paid as much as he did, to verbally draft his work so that the powers that be up the line from him wouldn't realise that he was a Luddite working in the computer age.

He was connected to the halls of power. He was connected up on the hill. It didn't do much for him when he got busted down from deputy head because sometimes heads roll. It did mean that often he would hear about things before some politician had said it aloud. Often before the agency head had heard about them.

Which could give us a head start on policy making but meant we had to suffer through him. Because he was connected and clearly had stopped caring around the time he stopped being deputy head, his uniform was jeans and a t-shirt. It was a ridiculous look on a man that must have been in his 60s. Made more so by his attempts to stay relevant with other people. Always talking about music and his record collection. Trying to connect with people over the latest films.

From how other people responded it appeared that his taste was decent to good. But it didn't stop the creepiness of a man who probably had grandkids trying his hardest to get in with the youth of today.

Sometimes I looked at him and wondered if I was in the service long enough, if he was my final form. At some point I would close myself in a quiet room. Hibernate for a time. Days, weeks, perhaps months, later I would emerge. I would have become The End. Designed to haunt future generations of public servants.

Compounding this was an unrelenting choice on his part to talk exclusively in jargon. He assumed that everyone in his earshot was versed in exactly the technical language of government that he was. Often I found myself translating his words for most of a meeting and missing whatever point he was making. I'd just nod because more often than not he was looking for agreement. I'll admit that sometimes I just started to thinking about anything else while he was speaking. It never ended well for me and I'd end up with the lion's share of the work on a project as a result but at least for that half an hour I didn't have to truly experience The End.

He also had a tendency to blow things up at the last minute. I once worked with him for a year on sharing data between agencies to support their policy needs. Memorandums of Understanding were drafted. Legal advice was sought. Hours of meetings were held. 3 weeks out from everything going into effect, he asked, "Why are we doing this?"

For a moment I worried that he had dementia and The End had finally cracked. It had been pretty clear for most of the past year why we were doing it. Over the next 2 weeks it all unravelled and I had other agencies hounding me for years after. Such was the suction The End had with those that made decisions. Of course, he was able to walk away and continue to haunt the corridors and my career took an enormous dent.

Sometimes when I see The End I want to kill everything he loves.

So to have Charlie say we were meeting with The End and he hadn't told me why. That put me on alert. My senses were heightened. If I listened carefully enough I could hear Charlie's hairline receding.

The End swept into the room and pulled up a chair. I always half expect him to sit on it backwards like a guidance counsellor that wants to , you know, connect with the kids.

"Alright. Thank you for meeting with me. You will have seen in the media today about IPCC 6 coming out. Up on the hill they're worried that they need to be seen to be doing something on climate change. So I need the team to come up with ideas by COB tomorrow. Remember, the Government wants to create jobs. That is the most important thing. If there's a need to ramp up an industry like renewables and that comes at the cost of the non-renewable industry, then you have to make sure that those jobs don't get lost, or they get transitioned to other industries, and that there is a net gain. Anything that doesn't have that is a non starter. They aren't going to care if there isn't a huge boost to the economy or it has a social impact or whatever. It just needs to have job creation."

Because of course they wants numbers to put in a media statement ahead of the next election.

The End swept out of the room. I couldn't bring myself to look at Charlie. Charlie was probably fine with this because it meant he could just pester me every hour, on the hour for the next 24 hours until me and the team had come up with something.

Some days I dream about the end of the world.

Chapter 11

There are some unwritten rules in offices. Lines that cannot be crossed lest some normally mild-mannered staff member goes on a rampage.

Opening the fridge, there is one of those fancy looking Japanese lunch boxes that are all the rage. Bento box style. A transparent lid shows a side of salad, a bed of rice and carefully laid strips of fish. It's difficult at this angle to tell precisely what sort of fish is on offer. A closer look with the lunchbox in hand reveals pickled mackerel.

The box has a strip of masking tape with the name 'Simon' scrawled. People believe that if you label your food there is no chance it will be stolen.

With the wholesale cultural appropriation of north eastern Asian cultures like Japan and Korea, there is a general acceptance that people can eat sushi in the office. Even fish based sushi. The portions are small enough that the scent is minor and doesn't linger. Particularly when being eaten by someone that will lavish coats of soy on the sushi.

However, actual fish. People will not stand for that. It does not matter if you eat it in the lunch room or at your desk, people will raise a ruckus for most of the rest of the day and if it is a pungent fish that outrage may extend into the next day.

There is even the possibility of a complaint being made to HR.

From time to time, you will witness quiet versions of this play out. Someone walks over to a desk. Hushed words are exchanged. You think you overhear 'union' as part of the conversation. The offended walks off to make it through the rest of the day. The offender storms to the nearest rubbish bin and with a loud thud throws the remainder of their lunch away.

The pickling on the mackerel is fairly precise, suggesting 'Simon' has tweaked the recipe over time. The smell of the fish escapes the instant the lunch box is cracked open. I empty the lunch box into the nearest bin, those that choose to eat in the lunch room can deal with the stench that will grow throughout the day.

Chapter 12

I don't know if this happens in other places because I have only ever known this place but every time there's a minor crisis or need to work something out we all pile into a room and waste hours of our lives. The sort of thing that could be achieved over email or just huddling around someone's desk.

While we waited, Terry was talking about his grand kids. Despite the years we've worked together, I don't know their names. I guess I just never bothered to learn them. I don't even know his wife's name. I know she owns a cup cake stall that they man at various farmers markets on the weekends. Some Mondays he comes to work and spends 2 hours crowing about how much they made on the weekend. I don't know how that information is supposed to help people.

Terry is the sort that will regale anyone who will listen, anyone who won't immediately walk away when they see which way things are going, with tales of when he was a young public servant and when we was first coming up. How he was a temp for 3 years before they made him permanent. How all the computer systems we have are useless and he designed all the ones they had back then and they worked. How he was a bag man for various politicians. How he used to travel the world.

Terry knew things and had done things. He wouldn't let anyone forget that. The sort of servant that had spent a long journey doing many different things to arrive no further than the middle of the service. He knew his stuff but couldn't convince anyone in leadership that he knew enough that he should be leadership.

When I first started and he was already in middle age, he spent a lot of time trying to mentor me. He never said that's what he was trying to do but he was clearly making a play to find a small place for me under his wing. He would regale me with tales of his time working out of the Japan office. Stories of that time he spent 6 months in South America trying to drum up business for oil companies here. That time he was having to advise one of the politicians up the hill in the chamber while an opposition member was speaking and his politician leaned in close to him and whispered in his ear, "What a cunt."

He would tell these stories to most people that would listen. There was a pace to his speech that some found alarming. A speed that suggested he needed to get all the words out because the person may walk outside of the sphere where they could hear him at any moment. You heard things about Terry that added to the picture he presented. Second hand you would hear that he was medicated for anxiety, that everything you saw, the words that just poured from him, his inability to move up the line after all these years was because he was just so anxious that he overcorrected.

The problem we have with Terry's stories these days is that Ben likes to engage. Ben hasn't been with us long enough to realise that the way to manage Terry is just to ignore him, walk away from him, or smile politely and use the down time to consider all the ways that you could make him disappear.

Ben seems to think that there is an alternative strategy, which is to talk more than Terry in the hopes that, I don't know, he might be so overwhelmed by your words that he'll stop talking? It doesn't work. What we've found is that the both of them together in a room creates a magnifying effect and what was Terry derailing the conversation for an hour turns into 2 hours.

Of course, Ben doesn't realise this.

I tried to start talking about the sign that hangs above the printer.

The sign says "Quiet conversation allowed in this area". Which is normal. There are all manner of signs in any office that try to restrict who you are when you exist in the office.

Only today, I notice that the sign is not just words on a yellow background, that someone has typed into a document and then printed on yellow paper. Instead, the sign is a photo of a sign that says "Quiet conversation allowed in this area" that has been printed on yellow paper but when creating this new sign, which is a photo of another sign, a red border has been added around the photo.

Which means that someone has printed this on white paper because if they didn't then the red or the yellow or both wouldn't print in those colours properly.

But at least it means that I don't have to listen to people when they are standing together at the printer.

Terry just kept on talking. James gave me a wan smile that seemed to be somewhere between "thanks for trying" and "that's what you think would derail him?"

Charlie walked in with a woman I didn't recognise.

"Before we begin, this is Sarah, she's new starting with us today. She'll be working alongside our team. Please make her welcome."

We all did a slight wave. A few murmured hellos. The usual greeting you could or should expect from a group of servants.

"Hi everyone, it's nice to meet you. I'm looking forward to working with you all."

It didn't sound like she'd been a servant long. She looked young enough that maybe she was fresh from the entrance exam. Maybe she had a doctorate. She didn't look so young that she was fresh out of university but add in a few years for doctoral studies and you could see it. Regardless, she sounded fresh. There was too much hope in her tone. There was too much life in her smile.

It was a nice smile. Warm. Open. Inviting.

I'm sure we'd get along well enough. I know how to be social enough that I'm something like friendly with people on the floor. Problem is, the smart ones, the ones with ideals, those are the ones I push up against the hardest. It's not that I'm consciously trying to break them or wear them down, I just find their optimism grating.

Charlie was back to talking, "The End has asked that we come up with ways the Government can demonstrate that they are taking action on climate change. With IPCC 6 dropping there's a feeling that we need to start moving if we're going to be hitting targets."

I'm not sure if he actually said it but it sure felt like Ben muttered "motherfuckers" under his breath.

"The End wants this done?" asked Derrick. "Not the head? Do we know this a real thing? Wouldn't be the first time The End has told us something and it turned out he just anticipated wrong."

"The End says it comes from up on the hill, that's all I've got, Derrick", replied Charlie. Charlie doesn't like it when we ask questions. Of course, when we don't ask questions he thinks we aren't engaged.

"It's just performative," I opened with. I could feel the eye rolls. 'Performative' had been my word of the past year. The first time I used it it went over well so I just kept using it. I know I'm at diminishing returns but I just keep using it because I like how it sounds when it comes out of my mouth. It had become a shorthand for just about anything the agency was doing, or wanting to do, that I disagreed with. The apathy I faced when I used the word probably wasn't wrong but then neither was I.

I think I may have said that last part aloud.

I was waiting for Ben to jump in. No one wanted him to but he was a bit of an expert when it came to this space so it would come as no surprise if he hijacked the meeting.

"And that's it? Just we need something for them, some climate action, or some demonstration of climate action? Brian is right, this is performative. Where do we even start? The End, man, we've got to stop listening to him," Derrick jumped in before Ben could fortunately.

"Yes, I know your stance on this Derrick." Charlie has this look he has been workshopping for years now. An equal mix of hating life and trying to be a manager.

"He mentioned that jobs is the main driver here. Any displaced workers need to be accounted for. They're not wanting major impacts on the economy," I chimed in. When Charlie wants to be on a beach in the Caribbean and doesn't want to do his job, 9 times out of 10 he'll leave me to do the heavy lifting.

"Sure. It's an election year. They don't want to take anything to the polls that could spook the base." Terry can always be relied on to tell us the most obvious thing. It just gives him a launchpad for whatever is going to spew out of his mouth.

There was an almost audible flinch. But then an unsure voice spoke.

"What are the current policy settings for the Government on climate change?" I made a mental note to buy Sarah a coffee sometime soon. I don't know if she read the room or she just likes to ask questions but she'd saved us from the single most interminable thing today.

"The free market will cure all ills," said James in the deadpan way he does. His eyes sparkled at me. I stifled a laugh.

Of course this meant that Ben had an opening.

"We've known what we need to do for years. Hell, when I was a kid in the 90s we knew what we had to do. We might not have had the technology or the resolve but we knew what was needed. You want to know what they need to do? Shut down coal. Shut it down today, or if not today then by the end of the year. Transition to renewables at scale. Pump massive amounts of money into investment in hydrogen and solar and wind and batteries. Set up an investment attraction funding pathway so the private sector comes to town. Cut payroll tax for business that transitions to renewables by the end of the year. Eliminate payroll tax for businesses that do large scale renewables projects. Bring in a tax on emissions and don't allow business to pass on those costs to the consumer. Provide a payment to business for each job that is related to renewables technology that they create. Not support, create. For workers that are displaced by the closing down of coal, pay for them to reskill, I mean completely pay for it, if they can't be reskilled then give them a package to assist with relocation costs and to find them work that aligns with their skills. Don't approve any new projects that are going to lead to an increase in emissions. Stop trading with countries that won't set targets to reduce emissions or that are still utilising fossil fuels for power generation. That's it. Done. Some of the technology won't be there yet, so invest heavily in research and development, give grants to universities that prioritise research in those areas. Set up clusters so business can collaborate."

He continued on for awhile. He wasn't wrong. It was a radical reorientation for the economy and it would never get up. But he wasn't wrong.

"And then they lose the election and the other guys come in and don't do any of that," I wouldn't say that Derrick sneered when he said it but there was the taste of it hanging on each of the words.

"Sure but…" Ben started.

"Derrick is right, Ben. That would be a non starter," said Charlie gently, "it needs to be something that they can take to the election. Something that clearly will create jobs but not displace people." Ben was something of a golden boy in the agency and Charlie was always too cowardly to properly come at him. You should see what would happen if I tried something like that.

Ben was almost vibrating. I was starting to get concerned that Ben might go on the rant he'd had with me earlier. There were enough people in the older generation in the room that he might pull a knife and start stabbing them for stealing the future.

"Then the line is just to target investment in new and emerging technologies that will lead to a reduction in emissions," Ben replied sullenly.

"Or we could just move the goal posts and start using

emissions intensity as the metric," you can always rely on Terry to know the jargon of just about anything. It comes in handy when he isn't drowning you in words.

"There will need to be a briefing note with whatever we come up with. Brian, you can get on to that once you have all landed on a position." Charlie never misses the chance to dole out work when required. It's how he can tell others he is a manager.

"Best get Sarah to do that, would be a good development opportunity to show her how the team's workflow functions."

Leadership will do anything to show they are offering us servants 'development opportunities.' Using the term is almost guaranteed to get work off your plate. Their worry is that without something that looks like progression, we'll start thinking about moving to the private sector.

There's always briefing notes. Always. We can barely buy a stapler without a briefing note to accompany it, justifying the reason we need another stapler and what we will do to offset the net debt impact to the budget.

As we shuffle out, I say to Sarah that she should send the briefing note to me before it goes to Charlie.

Of course, none of this matters. But I wouldn't say that out loud. You never say it out loud in the service.

Chapter 13

It woke me like a scratchy headache. It was 3am. I was in no mood to be awake. The darkness of my room enveloped me. I had the lingering aftertaste of a shout. Shouting in my dream. Like I had been shouting in the real world but couldn't find my voice in my dream.

An afterimage of a cold empty universe stretching out in front of me took a moment to shake. Crystalline. The word hung in my head. Crystalline. Rolled around on my tongue. Crystalline.

A shout in the space between reality and the unreality of the dream world.

Something out there. That couldn't be seen but could be felt.

A cold presence.

The source of the shouting.

I rolled over and went back to sleep.

My alarm woke me again. As it always does.

My morning routine was without note.

The walk to the train station was filled with a podcast about the rise of neo fascists in Eastern Europe. My noise cancelling headphones ensured that I noticed nothing different about the world.

The 6.45am train into the city is haunted by the unawake.

Eye contact is unwelcome. Talking is verboten. No one notices anything of their fellow passengers. This is the way it is. This is the way it should be.

And so there was no chance I would notice anything different about the world.

The wind howled as I stepped off the elevator into the office.

Dark clouds sat outside the window. The weather had been strange all year.

James sat at his computer as if he couldn't hear the wind whipping outside.

I grunted a good morning at him, not trying to hide my displeasure that he had beaten me into the office.

He jerked a thumb towards the window.

"Terry," he said in return greeting.

Following the line of his thumb, I noticed the Terry sized hole in the window. The wind tore at papers in binders on the window sill.

HR would probably need to fill out, at minimum, three forms and write two briefing notes about this.

"Have you read yesterday's Hansard?" James asked. "Ben isn't going to be happy."

Chapter 14

You never want to be asked if you've read yesterday's Hansard.

It will often mean that out masters on the hill have said something stupid. Or announced something that no one has any idea about. Or misrepresents something you have been pulling together for the past six months.

Whatever it is, it means that work is coming for you. That Charlie will appear at your shoulder to pull you into a room.

Because it will be your fault. Our masters on the hill are just voices for us. So if something is wrong then it is something you have done.

And if they announce something that no one knows about. Well, that means you have to reverse engineer the future. When you can't do that because no one can do that, you will find Charlie at your shoulder.

I didn't want to deal with Hansard this morning. I wasn't shaken by Terry. That wouldn't be the word. I was in a fugue. It was the thread that broke my routine.

I would shed no real tears over Terry. Not that I had anything against the man. He was pleasant if vacuous.

It just made my mind shout, "None of this matters!"

Why should I worry about Hansard and the words of our masters?

It must be about IPCC 6. I need coffee before that. The way our masters talk in Hansard is like reading Shakespeare. I need to read it four times to get what they're saying. And another two times to get what this is going to mean for my day (if not month or year).

Coffee downed, I sat down to read Hansard. It always takes me awhile to find it. James could have told me which page but that would have saved me scrolling through pages of chatter about puppy farming and railways.

Every once in a while I will get completely absorbed in Hansard. Will lose the first hour or more of my day, pouring over something that has nothing to do with the agency or my role.

It didn't take me too long to find what James wanted me to see.

Ben wasn't going to be impressed. But he had called it. The policy was going to be that we would have targeted investment in new and emerging technologies to meet emissions reduction targets (which were of course, yet to be defined, because politicians love to punt something if they can).

The End had, as he often did, wasted our time. And this was what they came up with. This is what they thought they could take to the election when the other side was going to run a full court press after the Government had been in power for 6 years.

Of course, that didn't mean that Charlie wasn't going to appear at my shoulder suddenly and try and railroad me into another meeting about this. I could already see the things that were going to fall out of the 'new and emerging technologies' comment.

We were going to have run some sort of funding round to

support it. We were still going to have to work out what to do with displaced workers. It was weak policy but that didn't mean there wasn't going to be work.

"Charlie in yet?" I asked. I like to think it was casually but I suspect James could read the nature of the question. He was good at telling when I was caring too much.

"Haven't seen him yet. His calendar doesn't have anything in it so he could be around."

I didn't have much time. I needed to fill up my calendar quick. It was too early to start reaching out to other agencies and the people I knew there. Middle of the day is fine for that sort of thing, you can quickly hustle a catch up with another bored servant. Most people wouldn't be in their offices yet. I looked out across the floor. Hardly anyone was in. I could see that James had grabbed his coffee. The paper cup was sitting next to his keyboard. Even Claire wasn't in yet and I could have suffered through a chat with her if it meant that Charlie didn't appear next to me and drop this all on my lap.

It was all for nought. As I turned to check the other end of the floor, Charlie was there.

"So I'm sure you've seen Hansard?" as if this was an innocent inquiry. Did he read it on the train ride in? Is that how he thought he'd get a promotion?

"I don't know if you've had any thoughts about it yet but on the train ride in I was thinking we're going to have to get the team together again. Maybe leave Ben out, I didn't find his input helpful."

Because of course, it would be me that organises the meeting. It could never be him that organises it. That way, when it goes south, people will remember that it was me that pulled everyone together.

Ben wasn't going to be impressed and it didn't make sense for him not to be in the room. It was going to be me that had to tell him as well. But it wouldn't be the first time I've thrown Charlie under a bus. Not that such efforts had achieved anything over the years.

"Sure, yeah, I'll get everyone together. Might need to be tomorrow morning though as Derrick is at that conference today and James is swamped."

With a bit of luck, I might be able to come down with some rare fleshing eating disease that would keep me out of the office for the next two weeks and I wouldn't have to deal with the meeting. Of course, Charlie would probably want me to remote in.

"You seen Terry this morning?" Charlie asked.

Chapter 15

People often make the mistake of assuming that the wrapping on a lunch provides an indication of the quality of the food. It could be a meal that they slaved over the night before which puts all other meals in the fridge to shame but they simply throw it in a sandwich bag in the hopes there will be a clean plate floating around the lunch room when they finally take their lunch break.

Take this sandwich for example. Wrapped hastily in cling film. Clearly done as they were running out of the house this morning, their children screaming at them as they kicked them off in the hopes that one of them wouldn't get their fingers trapped in the door again. The other week had been a nightmare when one of the kids ended up having to go to emergency with a broken finger because in the rush to get out the door while trying to remove the child from their leg they had all too quickly shut the door to the sound of a sickening crunch. The child hasn't trusted them since, a fearful look in the child's eyes whenever they raise their voice ever so slightly to say that the television needs to be turned off because it is bed time.

And with that wrapping, most people wouldn't give it a second glance. But take a closer look. That's a schnitzel hiding in that bun. Perhaps veal. Perhaps chicken. The bun looks to be from some artisanal bakery that has some hip name that is probably two suburbs over from where they live but they go there on the weekends to feel like they are cultured. There are seeds in the bun, it looks hand rolled and baked to perfection. The schnitzel itself looks to have been pan fried rather than oven cooked, slight scorching on the crust the give away.

See the homemade slaw that tops the meat. You don't get slaw like that from a store. At least not a store you should be shopping at on a servant's wage. A slice of cheese peaks out from the edges of the bun. It looks to be cheddar but the slight crumble to it means it is aged well not pre-sliced from a packet.

What you can't see but what fills the mouth is a spicy mayonnaise, orange tinted in colour. Perhaps a blend of mayonnaise and sriracha sauce, that sits on top of the slaw and seeps down on to the schnitzel. Which is chicken by the way. All in all, this is a person that knows how to construct a lunch time sandwich. The sort of thing that doesn't turn by the time lunch arrives. The bun, crunchier than it appeared, stills holds up despite being next to the mayonnaise.

And after all that, only a ball of cling film to toss into a waste paper basket.

Chapter 16

Claire didn't come in that morning. She rang Charlie and said she felt like she had the worst migraine she'd ever had. She had a moment yesterday where she tried to eat fish cakes that ended with her crying in a quiet room.

A lot of people didn't come in that morning. The floor was half empty. It was pleasant. James and I spent most of the day just chatting about nothing because there wasn't much else to do.

Every once in a while Charlie walked over to our row of desks and looked like he wanted to say something. Then he'd just walk back to his desk without so much as muttering.

He hadn't taken the news of Terry's demise well. It wasn't a dramatic reaction because Charlie wasn't a dramatic kind of guy. He was the human equivalent of beige trending towards beige and salmon mixed together when he felt stressed.

But I had seen the beginnings of some tears in his eyes as I told him that the gaping hole in the window was the silhouette of Terry and that Terry's body was down on the pavement below. Charlie and Terry had known one another for decades. You wouldn't call them close, and in private conversation Terry had nothing good to say about Charlie. They were civil and had a tendency to make one another laugh in meetings. They were clearly from similar demographics so there was a shared understanding of the world between them.

When you're not that close to someone who dies, you don't know how you are allowed to react. If it's a family member, or family members, then you get to curse the gods. If it's someone far removed then you just shrug, maybe mutter "that's sad" and move on. In between those poles though, people seem to freeze. Was Terry close enough that Charlie could shed a tear? Maybe. Charlie didn't seem to know though. He seemed to want to say something to me and James about it but didn't have the courage for it.

Eventually, when the day was almost done, he finally spoke.

"Did you organise that meeting? I think we need to move on this pretty quickly. They'll be asking for our plans on it soon."

And he went to move back to his desk but stopped. I was fully braced for whatever words he had been drafting in his head all day about Terry. Perhaps it would be a lament of a man gone too soon. Maybe he would ask if we wanted to go to the bar after work to have a drink in Terry's honour. I did not and Terry wouldn't have wanted us to but I would because that is the done thing.

"Last night... this morning actually," he started. Then stopped again. He wasn't facing us but was clearly talking to us. "I woke up. Or was woken up. I'm not sure."

My brain felt weird. Like it was humming.

"I felt cold. I'm..." he said. "It sort of hurt my head. Or I had a headache. I'm not sure if I woke up with it. It sorted of sounded like words. Like when you're standing far away from someone and you only barely hear them but you know what they said. It was just a dream I guess. But it was very strange, I've never felt anything like that before."

James looked hard at me and said, "Into the black."
That distant scream that I thought was my own voice.
A visible tremor went through Charlie.
"Something like that."
Then he walked back to his desk.

Chapter 17

She had been feeling warm for two days now. Her daughter had an ear ache. Complaining of it in the middle of the night while her husband slept soundly. It was probably whatever was causing that. She'd try and get a doctor's appointment. Was getting harder to get them these days, always seemed that once you were sitting there telling the doctor your symptoms that they'd cleared up a week before.

Warmth aside, she felt alive. There was a buzz to her that hadn't been there in some time. Maybe since he daughter was born. Back when her husband used to stir things in her and she would spend long nights out on the town.

There was a whisper she couldn't make out at the base of her skull. It felt like buzzing but were words. Had started the other night when she woke startled in bed. Her husband had been sitting up, head in hands. She looked at him and almost asked what was happening but after a moment he lay down and went back to sleep.

Since then the days had danced. The daily routine brought her joy. She would stop once in awhile and listen to the sounds that were coming from outside her that it didn't seem like anyone else could hear. The air shimmered.

A week ago she had been on the verge of walking out the

door. Tears in her eyes most nights. Her daughter's incessant questions pushing her to the brink. Her husband's hands crawling on her skin at night repulsing her.

Now, she felt like there was purpose. Her husband's hands still felt like alien fish that probed unwanted at her but she spent the evenings on the couch with her daughter having cuddles and watching nonsensical children's television. She laughed.

She was cooking again. Something she hadn't been able to bring herself to do in months. It had been unending toast and baked beans and her husband would find something to eat.

Sometimes a headache like fire would start near her chin and push back into her skull. A fire rushing up and consuming her. It would make her smile.

Staring out the window at the tranquil middle of the day neighbourhood, a voice spoke to her.

"Into the black. You will find me," it said for her ears alone. She smiled.

Her husband would be back from work in three hours. She needed to pick her daughter up from day care in an hour and a half.

The closet was full of clothes that indicated a fading life. Function and comfort rather than fit. She went to the gym regularly and had dropped the baby weight quickly. She'd hoped that her husband wouldn't just see her as a cow that existed to feed their child. Then she's realised that she didn't care for his touch. The workouts helped to keep her centred.

Clothes into a bag. Enough to last a week. Function. No point in that one dress that she'd wear on a night out. It wasn't needed. Not for what the call wanted from her.

Vibrations started at her toes and came flooding up her body.

Warm tingles. A gift.

From the kitchen, a knife. A moment to sharpen.

Tapping the knife against her Caesar scar. Grabbing the bag. Walking into the world. Alive.

She would find people and lead them into the black.

Chapter 18

In bars near the office, I could see the early finishers make their orders. Groups of work friends sitting on chairs and lounging on couches. It all looked warm.

I told myself that even if he wouldn't have wanted me to, it was to commemorate Terry's memory. That I would be doing a good thing if I sat and had a beer and stared emptily at whoever was behind the bar. I decided against it. There was no point, no reason to go in there and waste my time.

On the street heading towards the train station there was an odd sensation in the air. Faces seemed blanker than normal. Like their features were trying to escape their skin.

My eyes refused to work properly as I walked near the entrance. Looking around for what could be causing this sensation, there was nothing obviously out of the ordinary. My eyes felt as though they were being drawn away from looking at something. I felt nauseated.

Dogs know when it is going to storm. Birds know which way the weather is going. Our reptilian brains do something similar. We can sense when there is something alien hanging in the air.

There was tension.

This time of the day it's all commuters so it isn't like there was the sort of person that would snap and starting screaming about Jesus or the robots living inside them or how the Government doesn't want us to know the truth. Commuters are the sort that just want to get home and not get bothered. The sort that cast sidelong glances when someone talks too loudly on the train. The sort that would be anywhere else if they could.

You could almost taste the tension but no one was acting on it.

I felt warm and prickly.

I waited on the platform for something to break out.

I cast my glances up and down the platform. Trying to block out the world but desperate to not miss what I was sure was going to take place.

But nothing happened. The train came and we all shuffled on.

I stared at the advertisements that ran the length of the carriage. Not because I was in the marketplace for any of the things being sold but because I needed something to do and trying to read the fine print on an ad can often make you look like you're thinking.

I got home without incident and the day started to wash away.

I started my nightly routine of heating my frozen meal.

A couple of episodes of television. The South Korean parliament had just passed a motion of no confidence and it looked like they would be going to the polls.

If only the real world was that exciting and governments could be toppled just by a corruption scandal. Most of the time being corrupt made the papers and then everyone forgot why they had been so focused on that politician for awhile.

I don't understand why this show was a hit. It was so wonkish. You get shows like this sometimes where it's a comedy, and oh ho ho aren't those policy wonks hilarious and so out of touch with reality. But this was a straight drama that seemed like an indictment of South Korean politics. I'd have to check with the Trade team on how accurate it was but it seemed like something that was unlikely to break out from the South Korean market.

Strange times.

Then it was time to wander the internet and try and complete the set of ceramic espresso cups that I have. Check in on my favourite cam girls. And then to sleep.

Before I could drop off, I wondered if Charlie's dream was a coincidence. I mean, it's that time of the year at work where we're all feeling a little under the pump and maybe we're all just having stress dreams. But James' words. Those words I heard. The look on his face. Staring right into me. Unflinching. Trying to gauge my reaction.

Into the black.

There was more to it but all I had was the aftertaste of that moment when I woke. Not a dream. Something from outside me. Something that happened physically. Or at least something that happened psychically that I felt physically.

I closed my eyes and breathed. There was nothing more to do but sleep and wait for the routine to begin anew tomorrow.

Chapter 19

Each morning as I have my coffee, assuming I'm not hijacked by some servant looking to air their grievances too early in the morning, I read through the summaries of talk back radio and press clippings. Most mornings swing wildly between grim and dull but it gives my brain some time to get into gear before the rest of the team are in the office and I have to be functional.

The radio news this morning is peppered with stories about increased mental health presentations. Not our problem, that would be Health. A completely different agency. But you need to pay attention to trends like this because it could play out in unexpected ways. A mental health crisis leads to a lack of confidence in the Government which leads to a mad rush to get something in place, some policy or project, to soothe their souls while their family members and friends are having psychotic breaks.

I make a note of it and go back to my coffee. There isn't much about IPCC or the stance on emissions. Stories like that take a day or two to get much air time and rely on the opposition using them as a cudgel to beat the Government with.

So you write some briefing notes and you try and come up with a way of getting through the day that doesn't involve you sighing every minute.

Then James says, "The Man is going to be holding a press conference."

Capital T. Capital M. You can hear the capitalisation as he speaks.

Which of course is enough to send the office into a spin. Politicians hold all sorts of press conferences most days of the week. But when it's The Man, our fearless leader, the head of the men up on the hill, then we have to pay attention.

More than a passing remark for tomorrow's Hansard. More than a cabinet level request for information. A press conference from The Man will lead to work.

There's a television that isn't turned on except for The Man's pressers. You would think we would have it playing at all hours to see how policies are being received or if we need to pivot. Honestly, we don't care for those things. But The Man, when he talks, we listen. And if we don't, we get caught out.

"What time is it?" I ask. I'll have to shuffle my morning around whenever it is. I might not cancel a meeting that I've got but I probably won't pay much attention in the meeting.

"10.30 this morning."

The earlier a presser, the more pressing the issue. This rates as moderate. If it was first thing when I got into the office it would probably mean that the hill was on fire and couldn't we all just think of the politicians. 10.30, it's more likely to be the announcement of some infrastructure project that they'll take to the election. Or their plans for emissions. Could be anything but it will end up being something we need to be across.

"My bet is the hospital," says James. Major hospital being built, many jobs supported. Plays well at the local level for an election. A marginal seat as well.

"Sure. But he'll run 23 minutes late as usual."

A wonk started tracking the time The Man ran late for each press conference for a year and came up with that figure. It became a running joke. And then a sad reality of life when you're a servant trying to plan your morning around The Man appearing on television.

We sit around staring at a television showing an empty podium and don't know what to do with ourselves. Derrick guesses at the press conference subject. Sarah sits patiently, her first time going through one of these. Ben comes in late saying his stomach is playing up, or would have said that if he didn't stop himself when he saw Sarah was in the room.

Claire looks as though she wants to mention something about Terry but as she opens her mouth there are looks thrown her way that stop her. She looks like she's in pain. Like she needs to cry out but she doesn't. At some point all of our edges get sanded down.

Claire knew Terry as long as anyone. Longer than most. Claire thought of him in much the same way the rest of us did. Her face did this thing where it looked like you smelled bad when his name was mentioned.

She was allowed to grieve. There was no doubt of that. The rest of us were not equipped to hear it now. Not when The Man was about to speak and we were going to have to work.

Instead she says that when she was in front of the train station on the way into the office she saw something that she can't describe. A growing thing that didn't look like anything she'd seen before. That she stood there for a moment too long trying to work out what it could be. No one listened. Claire just talked.

The lighting seemed to go wrong in the office. Darker than

it should be. Like when someone slowly dims a light switch to the point where start to believe you're passing out or dying but didn't realise.

The Man appears. Flash bulbs pop. A murmur among the journalists in the room with him.

"Thank you everyone. As has been reported, there has been a noticeable uptick in mental health presentations over the past 24 hours. We are seeing this across the board, and in fact across the nation. While our health system, a world leading health system I must add, is coping, we are facing the possibility that the number of mental health beds in the nation will not be sufficient. While this is a state level issue and it is the states' responsibility to ensure a strong health system, at the national level we are going to need to take steps.

"At this stage, we are unsure what has caused this increase in presentations. However, we note that this increase is being seen in other countries also. In fact, there is a uniformity to the increase globally that is perplexing. I will leave it to the chief medical officer to discuss that point further. What we do know is that there is a uniformity to the types of presentations we are seeing. While there have been times in living memory where we have seen similar rises in presentations, whether due to national crises like the financial crisis or epidemics like Zika, we generally have not seen presentations that all appear to present with similar mental health issues. This is obviously of concern to us and we will be meeting with state heads and reaching out to our overseas allies to discuss this element of what is emerging.

"I'll hand over to the chief medical officer now. I'll take your questions after that."

There looked to be sweat on his brow. He licked his lips

more furtively than normal. Perhaps it was just the lights.

"So it's Health's problem, nothing for us here," remarked Derrick. And he was right. There might be a flow on effect in terms of the job market if too many people were being hospitalised but we could get back to the grind.

Most of the team shuffled out, the news a small moment away from their day. Claire remained behind with me.

"I just, I don't know what to say about Terry," she said. It was almost a whisper she wanted me to hear but didn't want to say out loud.

"I know. I get that but I don't think I'm the right person Claire. Charlie knew him far longer than I did, worked with him a lot longer than the rest of us."

Her face crumpled like all the times I say something she doesn't know how to process.

The chief medical officer was saying there was an outside chance that the mental health presentations were being misdiagnosed and it could be a prion but they couldn't account for it being cross border and they didn't want to rule out anything at the moment.

It was clear that Claire wasn't paying attention and was floundering for the next string of words to say about Terry jumping from the 23rd floor. I left her to her thoughts rather than try and hear the press conference over whatever she came up with.

Chapter 20

"The Deputy Head wants to see us," Charlie murmured as he appeared out of nowhere next to my desk. There is a murmur he uses when he wants you to hear something but wants to keep it a secret from everyone else on the floor. He isn't good at it and everyone is tuned to the frequency he uses so they know instantly that something is happening. Ben sits two rows away and his ears prick up whenever Charlie tries it. A normal manager would simply ask if you had a couple of minutes and pull you into a quiet room.

"Like right now? Because I'm in the middle of something." I wasn't but Charlie likes to believe that we're all busy all the time.

"Urgent."

The deputy heads are on their own floor and not everyone can get on to it. It's yet another innovation that the agency has come up with to stifle efficiency and ensure we achieve as little as possible as often as possible. If any of us have to meet with a deputy head that we have to stick to Charlie while he takes us into the rabbit warren on the 22nd floor so that we can access the elevator that goes to the 21st floor where the deputy heads reside.

He wears a grin when we have to stick to him. This is how

he feels powerful

The 21st floor exists in the modern world. The 23rd floor looks like it was modern back in the late 1980s. The carpet is new but the pattern hails from the 80s. The technology comes from the early 2000s (and was old back then), and the coffee machine is a treacherous beast that is as likely to give you a third degree steam burn as it is a coffee.

But the 21st floor. Greeted by a perky receptionist. Air scented with jasmine. The toilet cubicles have space for two. The deputy heads get their assistants to get them actual cafe coffee.

Today, the receptionist wasn't at the desk. I thought I could see her silhouette in the conference room they used for external stakeholders. I thought I could hear her sobbing.

Charlie swiped us through the doors and flashed his power grin again. I'd thought about getting tight with the security guys sometimes just so they could change my access level. Not because I wanted access to all the floors but just so I could wipe that grin off Charlie's face. It would be too much effort.

Our Deputy Head was waiting outside his office when we turned the corner.

"Charlie, Brian, you saw the presser? Word from The Man's office is that they're expecting this crisis, yes - crisis, to be worse than they are letting on to the public. The health system is a shambles at the moment."

"Yeah, cause they won't fund it properly," I muttered not quietly enough.

"Sure, we've talked that through before, Brian, you know we're on the same page," the Deputy Head replied. "They're assuming that the system is going to be at capacity within 3 months at best. This is only for our ears at the moment, I don't want or need this spreading through the agency. You've got that, Charlie?"

"Do they have any modelling for that, or is that just hopes and dreams they're going on?" I asked.

Most Deputy Head's don't let people like me speak and we're just called in to nod along while Charlie and other managers are talked at by them. Every now and then, Charlie and the other managers need some detail on a question they were asked or thought they'd be asked, and then people like me would be allowed to softly whisper information in their ear.

Our Deputy Head though, he liked straight shooters. He said it pretty much every Christmas party when he would drop by for his scheduled 30 minute appearance, often with The Man at his side. So long as you delivered you could get away with a fair bit with him. There were downsides. His group often was investigated for workplace culture issues.

"They do. They didn't give the full story in the presser. By the end of the week they're expecting the number of presentations will mean that a majority of businesses in most sectors are impacted. Retail in particular. Especially because they expect to start bringing in some sort of health restrictions. We're not sure what that's going to look like just yet but it is definitely going to impact retail and probably hospitality. And that's just the start."

"So what do they think it is then? I mean, you don't get some mental health whatever, outbreak I guess let's say, that multiplies in such a way that it quickly is wrecking things like that."

"The chief medical officer mentioned that they think it might be a prion. That's what they think it is. It explains why people are presenting with neurological complaints, it explains why everyone is showing up with something similar."

"Right, right. So does anyone in this room know what a prion is?" I asked.

Charlie looked as though he was about to speak and then stopped himself.

The Deputy Head waited in case words would emerge.

"It's like mad cow disease, Charlie. Which means it's contagious, which means that the Government is going to be taking steps to restrict movement so that it doesn't spread so quickly. What I need you to do Brian, with the team, is start putting together something for businesses that are going to be impacted by this because we know it's going to happen so it's isn't if, it's when."

Because when you get to a certain level in the public service you spend most of your days speaking in cliches.

Charlie just nodded along because that was his role here.

"Do we have any parameters on this? Do we know what they want it to look like?" I asked after a moment of hesitation. Right about now would be when Charlie could jump in front of the train heading my way in the hopes of taking some glory.

"Just scope something and they can yay or nay it. We need it fast so we can roll it out at the same time they announce the restrictions. It's going to be chaos either way, we just need to make sure the chaos is manageable. I need it by close tomorrow. Whatever you can put together. I don't need it exact but I need something 95% of the way there that I can take up the hill.

"Before you go, Brian. I wanted you in on this now because we're putting you in charge of the team. Charlie, you're being moved to projects with The End. Before you say anything, Charlie, you knew this was coming. Right now, we need someone who delivers quickly and who has a good overview of what the team is on so that they can take them on and off urgent matters as needed, which is you Brian."

As we left the Deputy Head's office, I flashed Charlie my version of his power grin.

"You're fucking useless, Charlie. Couldn't say two words in there could you?"

Chapter 21

"I want to watch *Ninja Survivor*! Come on, Emy!"

"Mum! I'm watching my show, you said I could watch my show after dinner. Doesn't Ty have homework he needs to be doing. He spends so much time up in his room studying these days anyway."

"Emy, Ty, no one can watch anything at the moment. Your dad and I need to watch the news, there's something going on."

"Mum. Today at school, Becky was saying that her mum has been weird lately."

"Maddie, can we just… can we talk about this later?"

"Madd, your mum is right. We can talk about that later. We need to watch the news at the moment."

"But dad, it sounded weird. It sounded like Becky was scared. Of her mum."

"Shhh. We'll talk about it after."

News on the television screen. The family TV draws all the eyes in the house.

That presenter that David fancied and Jennifer knew he fancied and one time it had been the cause of an odd argument they had.

The chyron reads "Breaking".

"Breaking news, tonight. The Man gave a press conference

earlier today. A global pandemic may be coming to our shores. Here is what he had to say."

Cut to – Press Conference. The Man at the lectern.

"There has been a noticeable uptick in mental health presentations over the past 24 hours. We are seeing this across the board, and in fact across the nation. While our health system, a world leading health system I must add, is coping, we are facing the possibility that the number of mental health beds in the nation will not be sufficient. While this is a state level issue and it is the states' responsibility to ensure a strong health system, at the national level we are going to need to take steps."

Cut to – the studio.

"Sources within the Government have told us that while they are taking a 'watch and act' approach to the unfolding crisis, there is a chance that some form of restrictions may be brought in. Channel 17 News will keep you updated with the latest as it unfolds.

"Our foreign correspondent, Amanda Beckworth, is here with what the situation is looking like abroad. Amanda?"

David switched the television off. He rubbed his temples. It felt like everyone was looking at him. He was sure Jennifer felt the same way. The kids were spooky like that. Eyes that felt like they followed you everywhere, especially when Tyler was young.

"What's a pandemic?" asked Madison.

"It's nothing to worry about, love. It's just when some people get sick."

"Okay. I was saying, remember, Mum, about Becky?"

"I want to watch *Ninja Survivor*!" Tyler repeated.

"It's not long until bed for all of you. Emily, I know you have homework. Tyler, Madison, go and get ready for bed. We'll be up soon to say goodnight."

The kids upstairs, Jennifer turned to David.

"Is this anything? I mean, it's the news. And not good news either. I don't know why we're still watching Channel 17."

"It's got that show on sometimes that Emily likes. I like watching it with her. I don't know. I mean, did you see the whole conference earlier today?"

"Sure, I mean I kind of tuned out towards the end but everyone was watching it."

"Just sounds like the sort of thing that happens from time to time. I mean, he mentioned Zika. Do you remember that? Or, I don't know, swine flu. For a bit that was all anyone could talk about. But we were travelling on our honeymoon at that point and no one actually seemed to have the thing."

"I'm sure you're right. Do you want to hassle, Ty? Better you walk in on him than I do."

***

"I feel like I've been getting a lot of headaches recently."

"Me too. You sleeping okay? I thought I woke up for a bit last night and you were just staring at the wall."

"I don't know. I don't really remember. I don't feel like I slept well but I don't remember waking up or anything. Was there a shout at one point?"

***

"Breaking news, tonight. The Man says non-essential workers are to stay at home."

Cut to – Press Conference. The Man at the lectern.

"Those that can work from home will be expected to work from home.

"If you cannot work from home then you will be required to provide proof that you cannot work from home and that you are working in an essential workplace. We consider essential to mean places of work like hospitals but only for emergency treatments, grocery stores, petrol stations, fast food outlets but only takeaway."

Cut to – the studio.

"The Government has since published the full list of workplaces. Advice has been provided from The Man's office that if you do not work in a workplace that appears on the list then fines will be applied.

"Further guidance provided to Channel 17 states that one individual from each household will be allowed out for a period of no longer than one hour each day. During that time, those individuals may attend supermarket or other food outlets but upon concluding their transactions will be required to return straight home.

"The Man's office further states that commencing next week, schools will be closed until further notice. Arrangements are at the discretion of individual school at this time but they are strongly encouraged to move to an online delivery model for classes. Further guidance will be issued at a later date with regard to schools and day care arrangements for essential workers and should there be any revisions to the list of essential workplaces."

David considered what it was about the news presenter. The eyes probably. Combined with the mouth. She never stepped out from behind the desk, so he didn't know what her body looked like but those eyes shot through him.

"Okay, who wants to watch *Ninja Survivor!*" he asks.

"Dad, no one is watching that anymore. Have you seen *Ghost Fights*? Can we watch that? We get to stay up tonight because you won't be going to work tomorrow, right?"

"Sure, *Ghost Fights* it is."

A mindless show about ninjas that had been turned into ghosts that fought other ghosts (had they always been ghosts?) plays on the television. Tyler presses up as close as he expects his parents will allow. The girls sit, bored. Barely watching the show.

"What did they say to you at work today?" Jennifer asks.

"Let's go into the kitchen."

He starts the kettle.

"Sounds like there's no real issues for us. Sounds like one of the consultants heard from someone they know in government that this was probably coming anyway, so IT has been working out a way to make it work if it came to it. Might be a day or two before we can actually be back working but they seem okay with it as long as we're available if needed."

"Yeah, that sounds a lot like what my work is doing."

"So, do you want to fool around tonight? We could get the kids down soon enough and then…"

"Did they give you any sense of if they might start laying people off or anything? Janet was talking about what they might do at my work."

"It's going to blow over soon enough, it won't come to that. I mean, just because we have to be housebound for a bit, I can't imagine they will end up firing people. They couldn't surely, this is something the government has said they have to do, you know? But, what I was talking about just before…"

"No. Not with all of this going on. There's too much to think through with all of this. I don't really want to lie there thinking about all of that while you're thinking about Libby Whats-her-face from the news."

***

"Dad, what's a Shriek?"

From upstairs, Madison whoops.

"Like that, kid. What Maddy just did."

"No, Dad. Not like a yell. I know what that is. I've been yelling since I was a little kid, you always tell me that."

"You sure have, kid."

"The Shriek thing they were talking about on the news. Bobby in my year, we were chatting yesterday and he said his dad said its nothing, it's all bullshit."

A pause passes between the father and son. Cursing is unwelcome in the house.

"It's okay, kid. We're all pretty tense. I think Bobby's dad is probably wrong and it's a disease. It seems like lots of people are getting it. We just gotta stay safe and we'll be fine. Whatever all of this is, come the summer it'll all be over and we can go camping like you wanted to."

***

"Yes I am going out, Mum! I am going now. All my friends are going to be there."

"And if all your friends were going to…"

Jennifer stops. She's become her mother.

"Emily. I don't care if everyone is going to be there. You can't go out. We can't go out of the house. We have to stay safe. Your dad and I aren't even going to the shops anymore. We're trying to keep you kids safe."

"I don't care, Mum. It's been so long. I need to see people. I can't just keep seeing you and Dad and Ty and Maddy every single day. Every single day. I'll wear a mask and everything. I promise. I'll be back early enough and then you can keep me here for ages again. Please. Come on, Mum."

"Come down to the lounge and we'll put on a movie. Your

choice, whatever you want. We'll make some popcorn and watch something. As a family. Like we used to. Remember when you were all younger, we'd have movie night on a Friday? Like that. It's been so long since we've done that."

"I don't think Dad needs to be watching anymore TV, Mum. Have you seen how much he is watching at the moment? It's like it's all he does now. I come down in the middle of the day when I'm on a break at school and he's just staring at, watching hours of news. He has his laptop with him but I don't think he's doing any work. I'm kind of worried about him."

"Just let me handle him, okay. That's my problem. You just need to stay put and keep doing your schoolwork, maybe spend a bit of time with your brother and sister. That's what I need from you right now, Em. I'll be the one to worry about people, you just be a helper like you've always been. Alright?"

"Yeah, Mum. Okay. I'm just…"

"I know, sweetie, I know. We're all feeling it right now. It can't be much longer."

***

"Have you seen those videos of the people just standing around those weird looking rocks?"

"What rocks? I don't know what you're talking about."

"Didn't you see the video that Em was talking about the other day? There was a bit of one of the videos on the news last night."

"I don't remember that. I don't think I watched the news with you last night, did I?"

"How are the headaches for you at the moment?"

"Do you ever think you're hearing a voice from somewhere that you can't pin down?"

***

"I know you went out last week, Emily. We aren't stupid. I know you waited until we were asleep and the snuck out. You went to see that Stuart boy didn't you?"

"What does it even matter, Mum? What are you going to do? Yeah, fine, I went out. I saw my friends from school and we had a good time and I'm glad I went."

"And you saw that boy…"

"Yes. God. I saw Stuart. He was there with everyone else."

"We talked about this. You told me you weren't going to leave this house and you did…"

"And what are you going to do? Ground me? This is pretty much prison anyway. There's nothing you can do to me. Are you going to get Dad? All he does now is watch TV. That's it. And what are you going to do, Jennifer?"

"We're all trying to get through this. We need to get through this."

"I know. I know. I know. How many times do you need to tell me? I am here with the rest of you. It's the same day again and again and again. One time, I just wanted to get out and maybe feel like I was alive again."

From upstairs, Madison makes a whooping noise.

"What if you've brought it here? What if it's in the house now? What if Tyler gets it? Or Maddy? Or you?"

"Everything is going to be fine. We're going to get through this, Mum."

***

"Dad, the fat guy that sweats all the time is yelling on the television again!"

"Thanks, kid."

Jennifer leans on the doorframe to the lounge. Cool blue light bathes the room.

On the television, an overweight man, balding, yells to camera.

"This is Nazi Germany. This is the government marking us to know who will conform and who won't. You mark my words, those of us that stand free and will not fall in line. I will not fall in line! They will come for us. They will take everything we own. They will put us in reeducation camps. They will brainwash us until we are smiling little robots that will wear the masks and believe the words they tell us and say 'thank you, sir, yes, sir, more sir.'"

Jennifer walks over and turns the sound down, standing in front of the television. David looks through her.

"Tyler, honey, maybe go up and see why Maddy keeps making that noise."

"Okay, Mum. When I come back down can we watch a movie? Like we used to?"

"Sure, honey. Sure."

"David. David? What are you watching?"

"He's telling us the truth. He's a free man speaking the truth to power. This is all the things that they won't tell us. The real reason they are forcing us to stay at home. The real reason they are making everyone wear masks. These are the things that we won't hear on the news."

"Okay. I know that you took it hard when they let you go. It's not easy when that happens, especially when they kept Rick. I mean, Rick? But this isn't how you can spend your time. The kids need you. This is hard on them too. They need you to be more here than you are at the moment. I need you. Keeping the kids focused at the moment is getting harder and I still need to be putting in my hours for work."

"You want to fuck?"

***

"Mum! Mum! Oh my god!"

"What?"

"We just walked into the bathroom. Me and Maddy. Tyler was in there, tossing off."

"What? Like. You know?"

"Yeah, Mum. I do know. He just was standing there. Staring at himself in the mirror."

"Boys are pretty gross. You know that as well as I do. I'm sure you do. Did you get Maddy out of there?"

"Of course, I wasn't going to stand around and watch the show was I?"

"Well, is she doing okay?"

From upstairs, Madison makes a whooping noise.

"How should I know? Is she doing okay with anything at the moment. She's upstairs most of the time. She's always making that noise. She didn't seem too scared or anything if that's what you mean."

"At Tyler's age, this might happen sometimes. I'm not saying it's okay. I'll get your dad to have a talk with him about it. But for a while, this might be something he does and we'll just need to try and ignore it."

"Fine for you to say. When he noticed we were there he just turned his head and stared at us. He didn't stop. I thought he'd be shocked or something and call out for us to go away but he didn't. Just looked at us while he kept going."

"I'm not saying it's okay, Em. I'm really not. It's just a weird, gross age for him at the moment. It's confusing. All of everything else that is happening won't be helping any of that. I'll have a word to dad and he'll have a chat with him about it. It'll be okay. This will all be okay."

Emily snorts a disbelieving laugh.

***

"Daddy, there's people outside."

"That's nice, Maddy. Come here and watch TV with me."

"No, Dad, there's people out there. In the street. They look mad. They look mean. Becky at school was saying this was happening near her house last week as well. She hasn't been at school since Monday. Dad, come look at the people."

Madison peers through the venetian blinds at the window. On the street outside, people roam. Fights erupt. People scream. A fire burns in the distance. One of the people looks towards the house.

Madison gasps and closes the blinds.

David stares at the television.

From upstairs, Tyler yells.

***

"I've got the kids down. I think Em is reading. She seems to be doing a lot of that lately. I think it's probably a good thing."

On the television, a man in a caravan is pulled apart by a large monkey. Other monkeys stand around watching. They whoop and shriek. The man screams. Blood sprays. The monkeys bathe themselves in the man's blood.

"What is this? What am I watching? Why are you watching this?"

"It's good isn't it?"

"No. No! It's not good. You need to get out of this, whatever this is that is happening to you."

David reaches a hand out to Jennifer. She sits an arm's length from him on the couch. She flinches at the touch on her thigh.

"Come closer. I want to touch you."

***

84

Jennifer walks into the lounge. David sits on the couch, staring at images of men being ripped apart. Screams echo through the room. Tyler sits drawing. Madison lingers behind Jennifer. Upstairs, the sound of Emily's steps can be heard.

Jennifer has a backpack strapped to her back. She crosses the room to the kitchen. The warm light creeps into the lounge but can't fight the cold blue back. She comes back into the lounge, a knife gripped in her fist.

"I'm going out. David, I'm leaving. Kids, you can come with me."

Tyler looks at his mum and grins.

David doesn't move.

Jennifer grabs at her head. She grunts. A moment of pain. The others in the room have a similar reaction.

She stands. There is a pause among them all.

"Kids. Please come with me. Emily! We're leaving. Can you come down?"

The kids don't move. David doesn't move.

"Okay, bye. I'll see you. Kids, come on. Now!"

She starts to move to the door.

Faster than she can react, David thrusts himself at her.

From behind Madison pushes her. The girl's small frame not lending much weight to the shove but Jennifer still stumbles and trips.

Tyler grins. He runs at her prone body. Headfirst. A tackle.

David is on her. Clawing at her body.

Tyler raises his arm and stabs her stomach with the pencil in his hand. She kicks at the boy. Boots slapping his head. David presses down on her legs to stop the kicks. The boy still grins.

David's hands claw at her face.

Madison slaps child sized fists into Jennifer's torso.

85

Tyler pulls at her boots. One off. The other coming loose.

From upstairs, Emily screams. Screams. Screams. Her steps are louder as they rush down the stairs.

Emily comes through the door of the room. A ball of fury. She leaps into the tangle of bodies. She rips at Jennifer's skin wherever there is a gap between her father, brother and sister.

Nails dig into flesh. Purchases are found and skin begins to peel from Jennifer.

Jennifer looks up at her smiling family.

Chapter 22

They told us it was a measure to ensure that people weren't in close proximity to each other. It was an attempt to slow the spread of the Shriek. My theory had been that it was some additional way they could screw with us servants in that most servanty of ways.

Say you have 30 minutes for lunch. Now, let's say that the elevator that will get you down the 23 floors from the office to the ground floor so you can go and buy something to eat, or when the weather is nice you could sit outside and watch the river. Normally, you might lose a maximum of 5 minutes to elevators. So in practice your lunch break is 25 minutes.

But with the new public health measures in place, it would take on average 15 minutes for an elevator to arrive, for you to travel those 23 floors, and to disembark. So now you've got 15 minutes left on your break and it's going to take that much time to get back to your desk. So your choices are eating in the break room but everyone else is in there. Or eating at your desk. So they get more work out of you, or so they assume.

You could take a moment and realise that there was a clear incentive in all of this. You could eat at your desk. You could try and run the risk of taking a normal lunch break but if you caught someone that was looking to find room in their budget, it could be that HR was appearing at your desk to have a discussion about your attendance.

Under normal circumstances, HR wouldn't care. That wasn't the way of the public service. This was a public health emergency, though. The Man had said so. The security of the public service was suddenly less secure. We all had to do our part.

No. The incentive here was to rummage through the fridge in the lunch room and see what you could find. That was two minutes' walk from most desks. A minute, perhaps two, to search for something to eat. Generously, you could budget five minutes to eat this cold sausage roll (pre-sauced). Then back to the desk and you still had time to do lunch time things at your desk like online shopping and checking the weather.

The sausage roll doesn't make much of a lunch, the size of a middling snack. The pastry soggy. The sauce soaked into the pastry not helping matters.

Walking back to the desk, you pass people milling about in front of the elevators. Varied shades of frustration in a row.

Chapter 23

You would think I'd be happy. A promotion without even trying. After years of not being able to get out of my role because Charlie was above me, there was a certain mild delight at being able to move.

This was tempered by the reality of the situation. Not the growing health crisis that would likely spill over to the wider economy. Never that.

I was less than thrilled by the thought of my marginal tax rate going up. On paper Charlie may have made a good deal more money than I did but in reality, once you factored in the tax rate, I would better off to the tune of about 75 dollars each week. That could be some mechanical device that I could use to get myself off, or I could save that money towards a better television to watch whatever new thing was going to be the show of the moment three months from now, or I could budget for slightly more premium frozen meals.

But ultimately, I was getting a little more money for a good deal more grief on the day to day. There are certain points in the service where the shit rolling downhill stops. Charlie was that level. He had been ineffectual, there was no doubt about that. But he had also given some effort to be a bulwark between the flood of shit that came from the 21st floor and the team.

Now I was that bulwark.

Derrick and I had once attempted to work out the tipping point where you were earning enough for the stress you had to deal with each day in the office. We were younger. We didn't realise there was no tipping point and once you were earning more money, the stress accelerated.

Nothing quite like managing a team and getting to play them off against one another, I guess. I knew this team though, I had been the defacto number two for long enough to know their ticks and foibles.

Derrick hated authority in any guise. He didn't despise Charlie because Charlie was Charlie, he despised what Charlie represented.

Ben did everything he could to get in Charlie's good graces but resented him whenever he wasn't in the room.

Sarah seemed like she would be fine, possibly surprised. She didn't appear to have turned on Charlie yet and seemed like she was happy contributing.

James just wanted to retire peacefully as soon as he was financially stable.

Claire filled meetings with words that meant little to anyone but her and got upset when no one paid attention to what she was saying.

Terry, of course, had left us.

So it came as no great surprise when I came back and told the team what was happening that Derrick sneered at me and Ben asked what I needed him to do. I told Sarah to pivot to a briefing note for this.

When I mentioned that I was sure that we had done up a piece on business support when some years ago there was a respiratory disease floating around South America that everyone had thought was going to cross borders and turn into some apocalyptic nightmare disease, of course Derrick reminded me that he and I had been tasked with that. Charlie was often forgetful in his management, so we had simply run out the clock until it turned out it was just a heavy flu season on the continent, didn't put pen to paper once, and Charlie forgot to ever ask us about it again.

Chapter 24

That night as I sat at home, a mouthful of a satay tofu curry from some new startup in the frozen meal game, a chill came over me. More, it came through me. That feeling when you have surgery and you can feel the pre-op starting to worm its way through your circulation. You know your veins and arteries are always there pumping blood but you aren't so keenly aware of them as in that moment when the anaesthetist pushes down on the plunger of whatever liquid they're using.

That was the chill. Not outside but in me, moving through me. A worm that was trying to find a home somewhere in my organs.

Down the seven hundred steps.

I felt like I lost a moment of time. When I came back it felt like an age had passed and my body had moved on without me. A disassociation. Jamais vu. A situation I had never been in before.

And then the South Korean political drama cut to a breaking news chyron.

An empty podium.

A sign language interpreter standing off to one side looking uncomfortable.

A scroll of text reading, "The Man is expected to speak soon."

A large text block saying, "Live."

As though they would broadcast something like this if it wasn't.

And some 23 minutes later, The Man came on. His face looked sweaty. Like the lights were on too high. The room looked too dim.

His face looked torn. That isn't the right word but looking at him that's the word that came to mind. Not twisted, though there was a hint of that. He didn't look like he was torn in an emotional sense but his face, the actual face of The Man, looked torn. Some psychic scar lingering on it, as though he had been wrestling with a bear on some astral plane.

And The Man, he said, "The early consensus is that this is a prion. We are going to move forward accordingly."

And The Man said, "There are some reports that this may be a parasite of some form. Our best advice from the medical community is that this is unlikely."

And The Man tried to stop himself from saying, "We have to take action. We have to take action now. From midnight tonight, we will be entering a lockdown period. This situation is evolving rapidly and until we can bring in it under control, we have no choice to take extreme measures to ensure that the least number of people, our people, are safe and healthy.

"Those that can work from home will be expected to work from home. We understand that this does not give much time for people to organise what tomorrow will look like both in terms of work and their home life. We understand that but people need to know that this is so that we can keep them safe. Look at other nations, look at what is already happening over there. It isn't just a dramatic increase in mental health presentations. They are starting to see steep increases in violent crimes. These are good countries, countries that have the same values as us, that look like us."

So not the shit hole countries then, or they were as well but someone like The Man wouldn't be able to tell the difference and he was unlikely to pick up the phone to ask.

"The violent crime is more than we would expect, it is different, it is startling. And we will not let that happen here. Our people will be safe from this. We will act swiftly to ensure that this lust for violence that we are witnessing does not happen here. My government has overseen a period of low crime rates, we have been tough on crime, we have upheld the law. That will not change."

And the sweat was starting to drip off his face.

"If you cannot work from home then you will be required to provide proof that you cannot work from home and that you are working in an essential workplace. We consider essential to mean places of work like hospitals but only for emergency treatments, grocery stores, petrol stations, fast food outlets but only takeaway. The final list of work places will be published on our website and will be up by the end of this press conference. The chief medical officer will have further detail on how we have decided what is essential and what is not.

"We know that people will be impacted by this. We expect that retail and hospitality will be greatly impacted. There are other industries that will experience a downturn. I feel for the people that work in these industries but I will not apologise for keeping our people safe. We will be announcing a package to support work places impacted by these lockdown measures. I do not want people losing their jobs or their livelihoods and I will make sure that the package we announce in the coming days avoids the need for that to happen."

Like that, we were behind on coming up with the package. Once our masters announce something, especially when they have nothing behind the words, there was no chance of ignoring the call of the office and the thought bubbles that would be floating through.

My phone started ringing. My days wouldn't end now. No more hitting 5pm and heading home with no thought of the office until the next morning. Now I was always reachable and expected to work any time.

Chapter 25

It was Geoff. The thing you needed to understand about Geoff is that he was a relic from a different public service. The service he had come up in was the service The End had come up in. A time when men were men and women were chattel and you could swear like a sailor so long as a politician didn't hear you (unless you were on the road as a politician's bag man, in which case you were expected to swear like a sailor just as much as the politician when they weren't in whatever glad handing, investment attracting meetings had been scheduled).

He was a small man and he acted like you would expect a small man that had gone nowhere much in the service to be. He wasn't good at putting on the facade of being a human being. Maybe he grew wrong over his too many years in the service.

This happens sometimes once someone has been a servant for too long. They become not a human but a creature of the service. Like a worm that has evolved to its surroundings. A crawling, beastly thing that knew nothing but how to survive the service. How to make the service profitable for them.

Now don't think I mean some straight laced corruption. Oh, this sort of servant would know how to pull the long con but they also knew that eventually they would get caught and would never get to properly enjoy their gains. No, this servant knew that the best way of seeing gains from their service were things that no one cared about. The drinks. The dinners. The access. The things that could be used as chips to trade with acquaintances out in industry. That may not directly lead to profit but could lead to the profit of those others, who would return the favour in kind with more drinks and more dinners until most of one's earnings wouldn't have to be spent on the cost of living.

The word that swirled around Geoff was that he and The End had been close once upon a time. The scandal that got The End sidelined had been close enough that it could have hit Geoff as well. But creatures of the service like Geoff were cunning and knew when to pull a cord and what bus to throw someone under. Geoff spent most of his time trying to get what he called kevlar. He'd laugh. He would work out where he needed to be and what cover he needed to find when the bullets started flying. The rest of his time he spent trying to work out how to take credit for the work of the people in his group.

Geoff was not well liked. Or even liked at all. He could be fun over a drink, the man knew how to tell a story and he had lived something of a life. But those on the 21st floor tolerated him at best. Some of them had been trying to rid the agency of him for years.

He was connected to a point. He had enough suction up on the hill that it wasn't easy for them. Showing cause had always been hard. He could present enough wins that the missteps he had made were tolerated.

Geoff was now my boss. Had been Charlie's boss. He was the conduit between my team and the 21st floor. Say what you would about Charlie, and Derrick and I had said a lot over the years, but he had at least acted as a screen between us and Geoff. That was largely because he wanted to take our glory for himself but it meant that Geoff had been little issue for us.

"We're fucked. You fuckers have the package ready to go? We are fucked. We are going to need this up on the hill tomorrow. I want you in my office first thing tomorrow morning and I want a plan. I want something I can show off down on 21. What have you got so far?"

"Geoff, we're working on it. We'll give businesses money to keep their workers on the books. We'll peg it to, we're still working it out, like 25% of turnover. They need to have seen a reduction. Or let's say they can project a reduction. Then they can confirm it down the line."

Because policy should always be made at gun point.

"That's good, Brian. That's good. Yeah, I can sell that. Maybe, let's make that 30%. Yeah, I can sell that."

I'd heard how Geoff would always do something to put his stamp on a piece of work.

He went on, "Okay, I'll see you in the morning but this is good. I feel better, Brian. I feel fucking great. You feel that. Can you smell that in the air? That's victory. They are going to fucking eat this shit up on the hill."

Which gave me enough time to turn the volume back up on the television and catch the tail end of The Man answering a question. You couldn't hear the question being asked so you had to piece together what it had been by the response. You couldn't expect a politician, let alone The Man, to repeat a question for the viewers at home.

But The Man, he was saying, "Into the black."

The sign language interpreter didn't know what to do with

that. Just stood their, staring, like they saw something a million miles ahead of them.

The Man was soaking. He looked smaller. Like the liquid seeping out of him lead to him losing height. He seemed further away than when the press conference had started. Like a dolly zoom in a Hitchcock film.

"The name that we are being told from other jurisdictions for this disease, this prion, is Shriek."

That's when we started to call all of this and all that would come The Shriek.

Chapter 26

The call came to him in his sleep.

An infinite voice. A shout he could taste.

He gave it little thought and went about his daily routine. A life that had been upended at Easter the year past.

Happiness had eluded him.

So when the call came, he was more than happy to abandon what remained of his day to day. No more answering to an idiot called Trevor. No more asinine conversations over terrible cups of coffee because it was better than being in the office at a desk but could still be called work.

He packed a bag and went to look for those of his kind. Those that had also been called.

He was not alone long. His kind could see each other in a way the unblessed people didn't see each other. He found family. Kin.

They lived together. They loved. A primitive existence that brought them profound joy.

They waited, anticipated, the moments when they would be blessed further. The divine fire rushing through them.

He was loved because he could find the forms out in the world. They would appear across the face of the Earth. Their leader, their Blessed Mother, would embrace him when he found one of the forms. A strong embrace. An embrace that told him he was loved.

They would live near the forms for a time, while they ripened.

She told the, one day, that there was to be a sacrifice. Once he had found the next form and it had matured. They would wait for the next passing to occur, so they were filled with the divine fire, and then the sacrifice would be made.

It was to be her.

They cried out. How could they go on if she was no longer with them?

She told them she would become one of the infinite. They would not be without her.

They cried. He wept.

Still he hunted for the forms. On a warm, starless night, he found it. A small bud of a form.

He dropped to his knees and whooped across the night air. The others came to him.

They would wait here. The form would grow quickly. It may not be more than a week before it was ripe. Then the passing. Then the ritual.

The others were a hive of activity, setting up tents near the form.

He remained on his knees.

Chapter 27

Despite the fact that I wasn't part of the agency's leadership, at least not what people think of when they hear that word, I managed to get myself invited to the leadership strategic conference that was happening off site.

During the day, those that had the Shriek seemed to be slightly more manageable. The off site was only around the corner from the office but I still kept my wits about me as I walked over. Plus the leadership gets fed well, they say.

I arrived just in time for the agency head to be starting her preamble to the session. Strategic vision. Mission statements. Good work of the agency. Time of crisis. High importance. Number one priority. The head had always been a bit of a blank for me. She was reasonably new to the agency and had been preceded by a man that was well loved by most. Her's was a different style of management. I'd never been up close enough to get a proper sense of her. By all accounts she was very well connected.

You didn't cross people that were well connected to The Man. Best you could hope for was a change of government, and that when the agency heads did their shuffle after an election she might end up at another agency.

You hear things about her. But the same could be said about

just about anything in the service. Half the people had no idea what they were talking about. The other half did but were frustrated they weren't the person they were talking about.

She passed things over to the consultant that was running the session.

Seems like too much of our time in the service is spent in non-descript conference rooms at off sites like this talking about things that could hardly matter like this. With the apocalypse happening, the agency coming up with a strategic plan, or whatever they were choosing to call this piece of work, probably didn't matter. Chances are that there wouldn't be civilisation left, let alone agencies, once the Shriek was done with us.

In the most recent staff survey, staff had responded that the main bottleneck to achieving in their work was that the agency did not have a strategic vision which meant they were unable to understand how their work fit into what the agency and the Government wanted to achieve. Or at least that's what they said in the numerous presentations relating to the staff survey. And then they would quickly, and quietly, mutter that yes they knew about the IT problems and were working on it.

Which all sounds like the words of servants that can't think of anything else to put in the 'any further comments' section of a survey they were being forced to complete, which people up the chain then took seriously.

You could tell the consultant was enjoying this work. Looking out across a sea of bland, servant faces. A smile crossing her face. This is the sort of work that consultants live for. You scratch the surface on this sort of consultant and you'll usually find that they were a servant at some point. One of the few that escaped. So they know the jargon and can speak that weird lingo that consultants speak to keep agency leadership happy that spending half a million dollars on this exercise was definitely, definitively, demonstrably worth the money and time it takes people out of the office.

Out comes the butcher's paper and it's time to do break out groups. I look around my table and excuse myself. No way I'm talking strategy with that guy from the renewables team that berates his staff.

I catch a few other knowing servants on the way out. Easiest way to avoid group work in the service is to excuse yourself and go to the restroom. I long ago came up with the story that I had been born with a rare mutation that meant my bladder could only store half a litre worth of liquid before I had to relieve myself, so if I had anything to drink any time recently I'd have to go. Of course, no one ever asked or stopped me due to my toilet breaks because no one cares enough to notice such a thing in the service. But it made me feel secure knowing I had that story in the chamber.

On the way back into the conference room I picked up my small box of food that each participant received for attending. I had heard great things about the food on offer to the leadership. So I opened the box expecting some smoked salmon blinis, or freshly made arancini, or those mini toast with a schmear of high quality cream cheese topped with some lightly blanched and salted asparagus.

Clearly the leadership was not eating how they once did. The box opened to reveal a small, lukewarm sausage roll, and half a muffin. I wonder if they had to buy them by the muffin and this was a cost saving measure. Catering packages will often list x of an item, I find it hard to believe that x was the number of half muffins being provided.

Still, the food would keep me going until lunch time. And the coffee they provided was decent.

The rest of the session was people shouting words out to the consultant to try and define what the agency did. Which seemed like a strange exercise given that it said 'economic development' right there on the tin.

And the consultant continued to smile throughout it all.

At the end of the session the agency head stood up and told us we'd all done good, important work here today and there was excitement over what the next year would hold. The other two at my table nodded approvingly. I just stared.

On the walk back to the office, I counted five separate fires burning.

Chapter 28

The nodules started appearing not long after the Shriek. Vicious, otherworldly coloured, scars on the fabric of the earth.

There was no pattern to where they would appear. Cities. Vast plains. Small towns. At some point, those lesions would start to appear.

To look at them would send some people mad. At first it was assumed that people were suffering from the Shriek.

For others, soft whispers. An entreaty would be heard.

Into the black.

There was one outside the train station across from the office.

It was of the earth. It was not of the earth. Some sort of artificial naturality.

To my eye it was a blob. Something akin to a haemorrhoid.

I couldn't tell you the colour of it as I had never seen such a colour. It reminded me of the infinite.

You couldn't look right at it. It seemed to shift out of your field of view. Like your eye was trying to escape its line of sight.

Coming off the train there were a few stray people that looked compelled to approach the lesions.

As the days went by more people joined them. They would

become stuck. Starring. Listening. To these cancers that were growing on the earth.

And as the days went by, these cancers started to grow. It was imperceptible at first. The way you don't notice yourself changing because you see yourself every day, then one day you realise you are no longer yourself.

The nodules didn't stay as simple totems infecting the earth. They started to try and take the earth back. Or overtake the earth. The scars started to encroach on buildings, eating away at the things we had built.

Still the people came. They prayed. They erected human shrines. The world had come to a standstill, they needed some form of entertainment, some kind of salvation.

Chapter 29

"We need to get something on paper and we need it this morning. I've given Geoff the broad strokes last night but we need it on paper for when I have to meet with him when he gets in around 10."

I got in early. Fortunately so had Derrick and James. Ben was a no show so far but he often rolled in just after 9.

"So what did you sell him on then?" asked Derrick. Derrick wasn't taking the change in leadership well. He had no love for Charlie, in fact he had often detailed fantasies of his to slice Charlie open from sternum to anus and hang his corpse out the window of the 23rd floor as a warning to other people considering leadership roles in the public service. But he had long thought that he would be next in line if something, like accidentally walking out in front of a bus, was to befall Charlie. He was smart enough to keep what he was feeling off his face.

"We'll give money to businesses, we'll get them to show or project a downturn of 30%, and for the money they have to keep their workers on the books."

"You supply side motherfucker. You know, you know because we have talked about this, that supply side never works. It looks good on paper and CEOs get fucking wet at the thought of it but the impact is awful."

"And I was the one in the firing line with a surprise call from Geoff last night. We talked about something like this the other year when Charlie wanted something, remember? So I went with it. We never managed to get anywhere with giving cheques to people, remember that was the idea, just hand cash to the public and hope they spend. And you know what? This is different. People can't go out and spend, we can't spend out of this like we thought we could last time."

It sounded like he audibly huffed but it could have been my stomach, I was already on my second coffee of the morning.

"I still don't get why we're in the office, The Man said everyone needed to be at home so I don't get why the head sent that email to you, Brian, saying we all needed to come in." Dependable James had always known how to defuse me and Derrick.

I'd received an email around 1am this morning. To all of the leadership. From the head. Word was The Man said the public needed us to be in the office. They had to see that the people that worked for their tax dollars were at their desks, not slacking off. Finding a way out of this or at least forward. I'd forwarded it to the team. I wasn't expecting Claire in, she didn't seem to be handling any of this.

"It's all bullshit anyway. This isn't a fucking prion. Or a parasite. You think we've all got fucking mad cow or something, Brian?" Fucking Derrick always pushing back. This was different though. This was feeling me out, seeing what I'd be like in charge.

"I don't know. That's what Health is saying. Who am I to argue with Health. I don't have a science background. You trust the science on climate change, I know you do, so why not on this? What's the gain here for it to be something else?"

"You know what a prion doesn't do? Or a parasite? Or the common cold? Or the flu? Or anything you would ever call a disease? It doesn't fucking hit everywhere at once, that's not how anything works. You have an epicentre and then you see the contagion spread. That's what SARS looked like. It's what MERS looked like. It's what the Spanish Flu looked like. It's what every disease ever has looked like. Because this is not some disease. If this is anything, I don't know what it is, what it could be, maybe it's some divine fucking retribution for treating the world like an inexhaustible money pit, I don't know but you don't know either. And they're calling it a prion because you know how you kill a prion? You burn it to the fucking ground. 1,000 degrees celsius. They've always wanted some way to depopulate us. This is it. They're using whatever this is to get rid of us."

Derrick was breathing hard. His face looked flush. For a moment too long he looked at the hole that had been Terry.

"Yeah, you don't know what this is so until the science says otherwise we act according to the advice and we do policy and we do the things that our masters want from us. You're not yourself, you need to go home. I'm giving you the day off. James and I will get the package written up, Sarah can lend a hand, you just go home and watch whatever you're watching at the moment, have a bath or something, I don't know, I don't care but relax. I won't cost you any of your leave or anything but you just need rest."

"Fine, sure. Whatever. I'll see you when I see you."

He shuffled off towards the elevators. Sarah was walking towards us as he left. That smile on her face. She nodded to James but had the foresight to see we were in the middle of something.

"James, you and I both know The Man wouldn't have said we need to be in the office. It's just that they haven't put any money into the IT situation for about 30 years so we can't work from home. We don't have the technical setup to not be in the office. Now, you write up the package and we'll toss around ideas until it looks right. Sarah, you can do the briefing note and we'll run the package past you as well."

Chapter 30

When the apocalypse comes, you assume that people will accept reality. Instead, people refused to believe what was happening. At first it was just the odd crank on talk back radio. You expect that people ringing into talk back will have strange, or at least hateful, views.

You get the usual lineup of privilege, outrage over what might be happening down the street from them, the fact that an 'ethnic' family moved in next door, that their tax dollars are being spent on something that they believe goes against their religion that they believe everyone should hold, that the politicians aren't doing enough, that the politicians are doing too much, that cheese doesn't taste the way it did when they were a child, that the air smells strange these days, that the kids and their rap music are leading to the fall of Western civilisation.

You expect that. Any given day the media monitoring summaries of talk back is filled with that. We send them around the office to make each other laugh.

But there was a hint of people not believing that there was a public health crisis. No one wanted to use the word pandemic. Not yet. Despite the fact that it was clearly global.

When the videos started to make the rounds on the internet,

the comments filled up with people saying it was all fake. The videos became fodder for office chatter. Claire was getting nothing done because she kept trying to show anyone she could the new video that had been uploaded.

Videos of people clawing at their faces. Videos of people strapped to chairs and being beaten while people cackled off screen. Videos of people whose faces were reduced to the musculature underneath where the skin once was. Videos of people fighting. Videos of people stalking people. Videos of humanity as it was now.

The worst videos, the ones that would shatter people for a moment as they watched, would be the ones that someone from the Innovation team would saunter past and say, "You know none of that is real, right? It's all been generated by an artificial intelligence."

"It's all been made with a generative adversarial network. The things that the university sector is doing with that sort of technology now, it makes all of these videos looks amateur. You watch, the next two, maybe three years, this is all going to explode."As days passed, the volume of people saying those things increased.

That the Shriek wasn't a prion, it was something else. That it wasn't anything. That if there was a rise in mental health presentations, and that was a question mark anyway because no one on their street seemed to be effected, that if there was that rise then it was because young people today were too soft.

That if there was a rise in presentations then it was because late stage capitalism had lead to a general disaffection in the population and maybe this was the start of the revolution. That it was people with head colds that had started to hear about this rise in mental presentations thinking that their head felt funny and they were all blocked up was actually them in a mental health crisis, and what they needed was to take a decongestant and get some rest and they would be fine by the next day.

That it was mass hysteria which was why everyone thought they heard the same things, like some sort of memetic disease had struck everyone and it would only get worse and didn't people remember other times that mass hysteria had caused entire villages to dance themselves to death. That it was a government conspiracy for reasons.

The videos were being made by some faceless servant somewhere to keep everyone in a state of constant fear. Even if people didn't believe there were real then enough people would that they would have their intended purpose.

There was so many reasons that not just the Government but all the Governments were in on this conspiracy. The point at which a prion can be burnt to death was 1,000 degrees celsius and so this was a way of governments being able to burn people, like in the old days when people they didn't like were burnt at the stake. That this was a way of depopulating the earth. That depopulation was necessary to mitigate climate change, or because with a smaller, fearful population the Governments would be able to enact proper control over people. That lockdowns meant that people wouldn't see what the Government was doing out in the world.

Claire was the one that brought all of this noise and refusal to believe what was staring people in the face into the office. Derrick would mouth off but he accepted that something was happening, he just thought they had decided on the what too quickly and the science couldn't have had a chance to deal with it yet. It was annoyance but at least I could keep him focused on the work.

Claire was the sort that would call up talk back radio on a regular basis. She was of the generation before us and had lived the sort of suburban, middle class life that left one with a blinkered view of the world and an inability to understand much of anything.

"When I say 'they' I mean the Government. Maybe not The Man but the people who are really in control of the Government."

I suggested to her that maybe she meant us public servants but I clearly wasn't getting what she was saying.

"No. Not us. How could we be the real power driving all of this? We make a difference but not like that. I mean the people that decide who is The Man this year and who will be The Man next year. Those people. The people that we don't know the names of, that are out there pulling the strings. They've released this prion so that we're afraid. Because what happens when you're afraid, you agree with anything that might sound like it will make the problem go away. You watch, Brian, they'll ask for our freedoms. They'll try to take our things. Our stuff. Because once they have our freedoms they come for our stuff next and then they'll round us up. Those of us that don't get burnt alive. You know what they plan on doing with the burnt bodies? They'll turn it into food, they're cooking people. They know we're running out of food, that we can't keep going so they need to come up with some way of keeping the rest of us fed. You watch, you'll see, it will be in the third world countries where the most bodies are burnt. You watch."

I didn't pay too much attention to what she was saying. This is how Claire can get sometimes, the sort of office person that thinks if we're all going to be stuck in the same location for forty plus hours a week that we might as well talk about anything and everything at all times of the day regardless of how busy we may or may not be and regardless of whether anyone wants to listen.

The rest of the team knew by now that you just let her go. We weren't allowed music in the office and silence could be unnerving, so sometimes you just let her talk herself out to have background noise.

Sarah didn't know this, she hadn't been part of our unit long enough. I could see her tensing. Her posture more rigid than she usually sat. Her mouth about to open to engage but I shot her a look. She seemed to understand what I was trying to communicate. She smiled at me for a moment and turned away.

If you watch carefully you can often see Claire talking out loud, not to herself but in the hopes that she will snag someone in ear shot that she can drag into a conversation. To experience the full brunt of such an attack can leave you withered and needing to take a mental health day.

She was mostly harmless, like most people of that stripe. All of this was fear. She was a good indicator of how people might end up feeling because she always reacted, emotionally, faster than most. Often that was a burden to deal with because things that had little to nothing to do with her would have outsized emotional impacts on her. But this was all fear. I wanted her to shut up because this wouldn't help anyone in the office.

We existed outside the real world, looking down on it from the 23rd floor, inch thick glass between us and reality and we could forget about it all and whatever we were doing and what impact that might have on the citizens.

This here, this was the real world finding a way through that glass to us. It was Terry's fault for leaving that gaping hole in the window. A hole that no one seemed to have any urgency to fix.

I missed a look that passed across Claire's face when she stopped speaking and I said, "I understand you're scared, we all are, none of us have ever lived through anything like this, the last time it happened anyone that lived through it would be dead by now. You just need to take care of yourself, make sure you're getting enough rest, if you ever need to talk or you need to take some time off, just let me know."

If I had been paying attention I would have seen her face twist for an instant. Not like when someone screws up their face in disgust or disagreement. Her features shifted, just for the length of time it would take to blink. Like there was something moving underneath. Or her facial skin was an entity outside of her body that was trying to find the most comfortable position.

All I was thinking about was how the IT systems had screwed me over once again and I wished we were working from home so I didn't need to speak to these people.

Chapter 31

If someone's idea of a lunch is a box sandwich then I can't find it in me to care. Hiding in the side panel of the fridge, I stumbled across two rice cakes, a schmear of peanut butter between them.

No one putting that together and calling it their lunch cares about the food. It is functional to a fault. Its purpose is to sustain the creator through the workday, nothing else.

Plus, one would argue, it is using space that is completely unnecessary. It does not need to remain chilled, barely being classified as a mid-morning snack.

Consider this stylish lunchbox of the bento box variety. Individual sections housing separate food. The main section home to sushi rice, topped with grated nori and a slight dash of spice. Another section houses thin slices of pork. In the mouth it is tender, despite sitting in the fridge, at a guess it was cooked less than 24 hours earlier. A hint of fennel seeds infuses the meat. The subtle sharpness of the sushi rice sits well against the pork.

The final section of the lunchbox holds a refreshing slice of honeydew melon. The sweetness of honeydew can often be too much, the sort of melon that appeals to children and is used as filler in store bought fruit salad platters. But taken at the right moment, the sweetness works to cleanse the pallet.

Whoever crafted this lunch is akin to a master. There is craft at play, a complete meal that takes you on a journey.

So you care. When this is what you encounter in the fridge, you take a moment and reflect on the effort and the skill that goes into preparing a lunch of this calibre.

It is the sort of meal that you must turn your head to the heavens and give thanks for before you take your final bite.

Chapter 32

It was starting to feel like my life was fading away from me in 30 minute blocks. Get to work, look at the calendar, see what comes first, what comes last and all the things that I'd have to live through in between.

When my alarm went off at 5am and I rolled out of bed to start my morning workout (to be followed by a protein shake by a company that had recently started production in a small warehouse not too far from the office and had been hoping to get a meeting with the Trade team to ramp up their export position), I would ask my voice assistant to go through all my meetings for the day and read any emails that had dropped into my inbox overnight.

That way, when I got to the office, I could hit the ground running. Some niceties for the staff out on the floor.

Not that anyone was looking for niceties anymore, you could feel the Shriek impacting people's minds, even the lady at reception had started to snap more than normal.

I had accidentally used some of the milk she had frothed for her morning coffee, not realising that she was lactose intolerant and bought her own almond milk in to the office. She had used to be a meek, smiling thing. Now she just about lunged for me, and I wondered if the Shriek meant that she would brandish a blade.

A scan of the newspaper. A glance at the media monitoring. Get centred and guess what was lurking out there that would derail the day.

First thing with Geoff. A bollocking. Some banter. And a request from the hill to reduce the level of the child care subsidy in the hopes of disincentivising parents from leaving the house for things like taking their children to day care or school.

A gap of half an hour to tell Derrick, Ben, Sarah and James about the request from the hill. No one likes it. Sarah starts in on what we already know. The literature says that incentives work better on people. At least most of the time. I tell them to get it written up. No need to overthink it or overcook it, we know what they want to do on the hill.

An hour with the deputy head. Some back slapping for the package. The Man thinks it will save jobs. The Man thinks it will save the economy. We all know it's bad economics and bad policy. But it's good politics and that's what The Man wants. The deputy head wants us thinking forward, there will be more on the horizon. Got to keep every dollar local. Got to keep every job safe.

There's a plan for jobs coming down the line. Something for the campaign. We won't have to work on it but it'll end up dictating what the work looks like for the next two years. A recovery package. The deputy head says that the Shriek won't be done by Christmas. The deputy head says the Spanish flu took 2 years to get done. Geoff says Spanish flu is a misnomer and it started in Kansas. Geoff waxes lyrical about why we call it Spanish and not American. I use the time to think about what I'll need the team to do if the politicians keep pushing for more.

Back on the floor Sarah has a peculiar look on her face. Something that reads a little too jubilant. I'm trying to scan over what the team has worked up.

I almost walk into the closed doors of the elevator trying to get to the senior managers meeting. I take the stairs instead. Down to 22. Tucked away in a conference room at the end of the floor.

The head of the Trade team is giving a presentation on the current export position. It's been trending down. There's a need for a push. There's a need to diversify the economy to not be subject to the whims of another nation. Everyone knows that the presentation was out of date yesterday. Everyone knows that there will be travel restrictions within a week. Everyone knows that supply chains are going to be disrupted and exports are going to take a hit.

Half the senior managers are checking their email while he speaks. Something like a third are looking at their phones hoping their assistants are going to call them out of the meeting any minute now. And the head of Governance is trying to get a sly nap in without the head realising.

I get waylaid by the head of the Trade team coming out of the conference room. His eyebrows seem manic. His mouth is too calm. I'd forgotten he was the next meeting. It's all well and good to keep jobs safe but what about those companies exposed to export markets, he wonders.

He wonders where they figure in the package. And I tell him we deliver what The Man wants, what's wanted on the hill. It takes longer than I feel I want to spend but he'd booked an hour slot and no one in the service ever let a meeting run short for fear they would have to be back at the desk.

I don't know if it's me but it feels hot. Everyone looks like they have a sheen of sweat on them. It works for some of them.

About an hour before the end of the day I realise I'd booked in half an hour to have lunch but all the meetings had pushed that back and I just manage to get to the corner store to grab another protein shake. This time the flavour is cinnamon banana (or 'cinnana' as the label reads). It makes me feel like I'm being waterboarded as I try to chug it down.

James asks me when we can work from home as he's walking out the door.

Derrick asks me when we can work from home as he's walking out the door.

Sarah brings me a coffee and tells me she's working late. She doesn't want to get on a crowded train. I tell her that hardly anyone was on there on my way in and she says she still doesn't want to chance it.

I ask her to tell me her story. No one ever knows how to start. But she gets going. Reasonably fresh out of university. High performing. Has travelled. Sounds like she's lived. Or knows how to tell a story as though she has. Halfway through I realise she reminds me of Ben. Halfway through I realise that I don't remember seeing Ben today. But I was flat out and he gets dragged into all sorts of things across the agency.

Odd that I didn't see any of him at all. I try to think and Sarah keeps talking. And I realise that Ben was at that conference about. About. About. Something. I'm sure it was important. At least he would have been fed well. And I realise that I kind of hate Sarah. In the way I kind of hate Ben. There's nothing wrong with anything she's saying. She's clearly brilliant. The way she talks reminds me of The End when you get him on topic and passionate.

Even though she's only just started, she already speaks the jargon. It flows from her mouth like it is her first language. You find that with people that have PhDs. They're trained to speak in a way that other people can't understand. That's how they're experts. It's what makes them perfect public servants. Almost no need to break them down and breed out any bad habits. Get them early enough and they'll rise through the ranks. Of course, the problem can be that sometimes they don't realise that the service doesn't care for outcomes, they only care about process, the process has become the outcome.

But the reason I sort of hated Sarah after listening to her was that she was the type that never realised when to stop speaking. That when she spoke of the things that she had done, the life she had lived, the cities she had ventured to, if you listened carefully, she was telling you how she had consumed experiences. She had not travelled to places like Paris and Tokyo and Berlin and Lima and Marrakesh and explored them or even just sat by a pool and relaxed. Instead she had headed straight for experiences that would make for good stories to be recounted.

In the moment it was fine enough, entertaining even, but given that the Sarahs and the Bens were the ones that I would eventually end up working for, I needed them to just shut up. And perhaps that was just what I told myself. If I had ever taken a moment to properly think about it then I would probably have to acknowledge that the reason I hated, even if it was only a small bit, people like the Bens and the Sarahs was because they reminded me of me. Except they were smarter, more ambitious and more likely to end up as my bosses.

All I had been trying for when I'd asked for her story was some sort of thanks for the coffee, and some sort of integration into the team. Not this. It was why I liked James. He'd give you just enough if you engaged him and not much else if you left him alone. But people like James, the quieter ones, would be the ones to snap. Especially now. Especially when there was something in the air turning people into monsters.

Look out the window to the street below. You could see the start of the fires. You could see broken windows. You couldn't hear the sirens but you could see red and blue lights racing from point to point. They would go out soon enough. You could see the start of the madness. A woman walked up to a man and it looked like she stabbed him. It was hard to tell from up on 23 but the way he doubled over, that's how it looked. You could see the people starting to come to the lesions outside the train station across the street.

Sarah, looking down at the street, next to me. She groaned. An odd noise. I saw her start to fall towards the floor. And then my head felt heavy and my body fell through shards of time cutting the air.

And the voice was there again. Calling me.

Into the black.

It was over and we were back up on our feet. Sarah stared at me. There was malice in that look.

"I'll see you tomorrow," she said.

I'd catch up on emails on the train.

Chapter 33

"Now hear this. They are lying to you, people. They are lying to us all."

Sucks in air, a heave of the shoulders.

"Today in the media, the Post, that terrible filth, they are reporting that the Shriek has been the cause of two million people dying since it began. I say no! No! There is no Shriek. They have made this up to make you sheep.

"They tell us to wear masks, so people buy masks and wear them. I don't wear a mask and I feel great. I feel better than I've ever felt in my life. I am healthier than I've ever been. I eat the food I want to eat, I drink what I want to drink, and I have never been healthier in all the years I have been on the face of the blessed Lord's earth.

"But they tell us that if we don't wear masks, we will die. That we will get infected. Infected with the Shriek. Just noise. That's what a shriek is. It isn't a disease, it's not something that you can catch. But they tell us to wear masks."

Grabs a face mask on the desk. Crumples it. Throws it towards Camera 1.

"This is Nazi Germany. This is the government marking us to know who will conform and who won't. You mark my words, those of us that stand free and will not fall in line. I will not fall in line! They will come for us. They will take everything we own. They will put us in reeducation camps. They will brainwash us until we are smiling little robots that will wear the masks and believe the words they tell us and say 'thank you, sir, yes, sir, more sir.'

"They are already doing it in China. They've been doing it for years. All part of a trial run to see how they can control people. I will not be controlled! I will not! You do not have my consent!"

Bangs the desk. Swivel to look down Camera 2. Pull back on the rage, bring them closer.

"You see, my friends, this is what they do. They manufacture crisis and they manufacture fear. They want us afraid. So we don't leave our houses. So we do as they say. So they can march us into the furnaces and we will thank them for it.

"First there tell us this thing is a prion. I know scientists, not one of them agrees with that. Noted virologist, Dr. Alexander Parker of the London Centre for Virus Research, a man that knows what he is talking about, said just last month that if this was a prion then he would resign his tenure. He is willing to stake his career on this. I don't know about you, friends, but I am going to listen to the scientists 100% of the time over the corrupted media industrial complex.

"Then they tell us, 'oh well, you need to wear a mask whenever you leave the house because if you don't, you're going to catch the scary Shriek, it'll come for you and all your family.'"

Wiggling fingers in a spooky manner at Camera 2.

"If this is a prion, then we don't need to eat masks. That isn't how that would spread. A prion doesn't spread that way. I've done my research, folks. I've read the studies. I've read the books. I've read more books last year than most of the so called journalists will read in their lives. I know what I am talking about here. The masks, goddamit it, the masks are so you get sick from carbon dioxide. When we breathe, that's carbon dioxide coming out. Has nothing to do with the so called climate change, people. Nothing. Trees love the stuff. Our bodies were made by the creator to feed the amazing world He allows us to live in.

"But when you can't expel that carbon dioxide, that's when bad things happen, that's when we get sick. We aren't trees, well I'm not. Maybe there's some bleeding hearter out there that identifies as a tree and goes out into the forest and just stands there. We don't thrive on CO2, we need to get it out.

"You ever have a panic attack? I used to get them all the time before I found Jesus. Don't get them at all anymore, feel better than I ever have. When you can't get enough oxygen and there's too much CO2 in you, that's when you get panic attacks and your heart starts racing and you start to sweat and you feel like you can't speak properly."

Gasp for effect. A beat.

"So why, goddamit, why would they want us to wear masks and breathe in all our CO2? So we're afraid, so we can't think straight. Some people, they'll get carbon dioxide poisoning, it's a thing, trust me. That can turn bad fast, let me tell you. People die from that. Everyone out there wearing masks, so they can say people are dying from this mysterious disease that we're all going to get.

"I hear you now, saying to me that it's not just people dying, is it? People are out there being violent and causing crime. Like that is anything out of the ordinary, that's what they've always wanted. Oh, that people are going crazy, they say. That mental health cases are on the rise and it must be the Shriek. Where? You tell me where. I don't see any of that outside. I've done the research, people, I've read the books. There's nothing out of the ordinary with mental health cases at the moment. Nothing that is more than other times in history. Crime isn't out of control, no more than it was last year when the murder rate spiked. The murder rate, the gun related deaths, all these indicators, that's what you need to look at people. They're all at the same level as last year or less. All of it.

"Have any of us seen this violence out in the streets. In the controlled media, it sounds like a war zone. I had a woman come up to me in the store last week, just came up to say hi and get an autograph. She said, 'where's all the bloodshed I've been hearing about? All this crime that is being reported?' and we both looked out the door of the store to the street and it was quiet. She was not wrong, people. She was not wrong.

"Where is it? Tell me. Where? Show me any evidence that the world is going crazy. If you can show me that then I'll see what you have to say. I don't mean these fake videos that they're putting up on the internet, the ones that look like some amateur horror movie. Fake, all of them."

Shuffle papers on desk. Pick up the sponsor ad copy. Straight down Camera 1.

"We are able to provide you with the independent news that we do, the way we do it, folks, because our great friends at Rads Away sponsor the show. They sell a great variety of iodine tablets. I take them myself. They've got a supplement I take each morning and night, called Men's Freedom. Has all the nutrients you need. Make sure you take it morning and night and you'll feel better than when you were a teenager."

Ad copy down. A smile. Slight shake of the head. Chuckle.

Ignore the sweat rolling down the face.

"Next will be a vaccination. It doesn't make any sense. You can't take a shot for a prion. You need to burn those out. 1,000 degrees Celsius. But they'll make us all take it. They'll say 'you need to have this shot because if you don't then you can't go to your job and you can't go where you want.' I'm a free man! I am free! I do not consent. They'll use the shots so they can track us. That's what this is all about. Knowing where we are all the time. Watching us. Waiting. And people, my friends, people will let them do it. People we love. Unless we can stand up and say, 'No more! No more!'"

Bang the desk.

Bang the desk.

"I cut up my wife yesterday. She howled. The scream on her. I never knew. I just never knew. When I was done I could feel a power rush through me like the wind does when you're down on the ocean."

Next ad copy read.

Chapter 34

I dreamt of nothingness. I dreamt of a door that slowly faded in from darkness. I dreamt of a gnarled handle on the door.

Opening the door, a vast cavern expanded out in front of me. There was no way of knowing the size of it. The horizon kept the edges from my view.

I thought I could see other people in the space but I couldn't be sure. If they were there they were less people and more shambling skeletons that moved to an odd beat that I could hear from somewhere. A light tapping on a drum pad, constantly driving me forward.

Wooden steps before me. They did not look safe. There was nowhere else to go. The door that had faded in from nothingness had faded out again. I was on a platform high above the cavernous space and the only way forward were the steps.

I gingerly put my foot on the first step.

It creaked. It shuddered slightly. It didn't look like it could take my weight. But it felt firm.

I started to take the steps. I started to count the steps. I kept losing track.

Nearly invisible to the naked eye, something akin to a bat fluttered up from far below me. It wasn't a bat but a thoughtform that had leathery wings and moved in a way that suggested it was new to flight.

As it passed me, it murmured of my day and the things I had not said.

The steps would turn back on themselves from time to time. As though a tower of sorts and the steps were limited by the space. Which made no sense, this space was so large that the steps could continue out in front of me to near the infinite and I was sure I would not reach the other side.

Another thoughtform darted for me. This one looked like a crane. A long beak extending out in front of it. I ducked as it came near me, my footing unsure on the steps which felt like they were thinning out. It whispered of actions I had not taken.

I felt cold but kept moving forward. I felt some fear from the height. I felt insignificant. A breeze blew from somewhere, cold wind against my face. I couldn't pin point the source of it or even the direction.

I wondered if I had needed to pack some form of provisions for this journey. I had no idea how long this would take me.

Ahead it looked like there was a large metal structure, possibly fixed to the bottom of the cavern. Numerous pipes of differing shapes poured into the structure from a place I could not see. They seemed to affix to the top of the structure but I could not see where the pipes could start.

There was a person sized hatch on the front of the structure. A small window on the hatch. The stairs took me towards the structure. There were railings on either side of me for a time. I did not know how long anything was taking. I seemed to be moving at my normal walking pace but progress seemed to stretch beyond my grasp. I walked towards the structure but it still remained far in the distance.

On the ground far below, I could see lesions flit in and out of the space. They hummed more violently then I remembered from passing them during the day. In those moments where they were existing in the cavernous space, I could look at them. Direct. They pulsated and swayed.

I could not understand why I could make out the structure so clearly if it was so far from me. I wanted to shout into the space but my voice didn't carry. Perhaps the structure was gigantic, left over from some civilization of pre-history made entirely of giants. It looked too advanced for that. Perhaps my eyesight was that of a hawk in here and I could perceive things from a great distance.

A thoughtform like a winged ocelot fluttered down and hovered at my shoulder. It urged me to keep going. To keep walking. It nuzzled into my neck and told me to look at the people. There was no one to look at. It told me that I needed to see the man inside the structure. It told me that I had done the right things. It told me that I had no need for concern. The man inside the structure would show me things and grant my desires. It told me that all of this would work out in the end. It gave me comfort. It let me eat from it when I grew hungry on my journey.

The structure grew no closer and the stairs started to turn away from it. The wood started to petrify and become stone. My footsteps sank to a bare whisper as I took each step.

After a time I found a step wide enough that I could lie on it and rest. The ocelot had long since been consumed. I felt heavy and a weariness come over me. The stone step was uncomfortable but it would do.

I slept for days. The thoughtforms came to me from time

to time while I slumbered. They would flit about and whisper their words and then leave me again. Then they stopped coming to me and I awoke.

I set out on my journey again. The metal structure was behind me, the stairs taking me away from it. I could turn and look at it but it was receding. It looked as though it was being kept at freezing point. Frost formed on its outer shell.

The stone stairs widened and each step became deep so it would take me two paces to get down each one. The stairs started to curve like a spiral staircase leading me lower and lower.

Whatever the light was in the cavern was dimming, an alien sun going down. There was no sky. There was no sun. Still the light dimmed. The world around me started to become grayscale. I could no longer see the metal structure. The thoughtforms were long gone. I felt the temperature rising. I could hear my heart beat increasing in my ears. My blood felt thick and heavy.

Then the light was gone and it was all darkness.

My feet kept moving forward.

There were still stairs.

I could not see them.

My feet kept walking.

I could feel each step though my feet sounded out little more than a puff of air.

And I kept walking.

And I kept walking.

Maybe this would go on forever.

The darkness was everywhere.

It felt safe.

Chapter 35

Two days was long enough that I didn't need to get a sick certificate from a doctor, and long enough to be away from the team and try and find some balance. I needed some of the 30 minute blocks given back to me. I needed to be able to think about lunch before 3pm. I needed to eat something other than what I happened to be able to grab as I ran past.

So I lay in bed and compose an email to Geoff and the team.

Something that sounded bad enough to keep me out of the office. But not so bad they would think the Shriek had got me and I would never come back.

Email sent and you sit back and wait. Knowing that within minutes Claire would reply with some too chirpy words.

But she didn't.

Sarah emailed in reply asking why I had sent the briefing note back to her if all I was going to do was correct some minor typos and change the date. She wanted to know why I would waste my time and hers. Once I was back I could tell her that if I didn't do it, Geoff or the Deputy Head would and we'd be caught in a cycle of the briefing note never going anywhere. Call it a development opportunity if you must. Whether she bought that would be a good gauge.

Tone never reads right on email.

I didn't give it too much mind.

If Geoff responded, he'd come back with both barrels. Head shot. How could I take time off now, when there were deliverables to send up the hill. He'd have to wait.

The time to just not be a servant. To maybe be a person.

Of course, after all this time, I never knew what to do with any down time. I was so used to the routine. I'd be on the train by now. People had been avoiding it as though there was a plague.

About now, I'd be getting to the desk. Thinking about whether to start the 15 minutes it took to start up my machine or get a coffee first and then start that wait.

Instead, I decided to take a bath.

At some point, I lost sight of myself. Outside of the office I wasn't sure who I had become. There was little in my life. Whenever I met someone new, if we didn't do the dance of asking each other what we did for work, I had little to say.

The work has consumed most of my apartment. Journals and magazines about policy scattered. A stack of books beside my bed, all non fiction and relating to the focus area of the day.

In the office, I was a leader now. I was the type that delivered and had success. I might not always do everything I could but nothing got lost in the shuffle. Nothing was overlooked. The briefing notes were tight. The policy what was asked for.

At home. In my apartment. Off the 23rd floor, I wasn't much of anything. A shade. A creature of habit that followed his loop so he could get back to the office where he became solid once more.

My apartment is small. I can keep the television on and hear it from the bathroom. The morning programmes were interviewing people whose loved ones had been affected by the Shriek. Describing the symptoms. I didn't need to see the television to hear the struggle in the presenters' voices to know they were affected and the show would likely be taken off the air in the coming weeks.

Those symptoms.

Everyone seemed to have the same thing happening. Their filter removed. Everyone their worst selves, if they weren't already. No niceties. No pleasantries. Unfiltered. Primal. Savage.

I didn't feel much different. I had been getting headaches a bit more often but that was nothing particularly out of the ordinary. A sedentary lifestyle. No use for impressing people. A diet that doctors had told me was an approximation of what a human being should actually eat. Too much coffee. Headaches came with the territory. And now I was taking it in the neck from Geoff on the regular, it would be strange if they didn't happen more frequently.

I didn't feel the urge to swear anymore than normal.

I didn't feel like inflicting violence on anyone. At least not outside the normal cohort.

I didn't feel like ripping apart another human to see what made them tick. Or taking the next woman I saw in the street into some dark alley to violate her. Or plunging from a roof. Or finding the nearest weapon and wiping out as many people as I could before turning the gun on myself.

The ultra violence sickened me. It was too atavistic. It said too much about what we were.

The people at the office didn't seem to be too affected either. Terry of course had clearly been infected. No other reason for it. No one throws themselves out the window because climate change has science backing it up. That can't be the reason someone chooses defenestration.

You wonder if there is any science to what you're being told. If you're acting on good information. If they turn to Derrick while you're not in the office and tell him that there needs to be a push to bring back the manufacturing of masks locally and whether he'll get right on to that and tie an albatross like that to you cause Derrick would think it might actually be something he could make his bones on, or maybe deep down he hates you enough that he knows it's doomed to failure and will eat a hole through your CV.

I'm not getting out. I've tried for years. Years. That stench of the service hangs heavy on me. I've been in it too long. The trick is to get a bit of the public sector shine on you, maybe a year. Two tops. And then go back to the private sector where you can leverage your tendrils into government and force them to pay you more.

Or you stick in the service and you climb.

And for the rest of us, we just float in the middle, smelling of bureaucracy and failure. Who cares what's lurking on my CV. If The Man thinks we need masks, I may as well be the one to foolishly deliver them.

The bath wasn't relaxing me in the way it usually would.

The sound from the television like a far off buzzing that wouldn't end. Just murmuring words and the occasional shriek when they cut to a shot of what the streets looked like.

No one cared about the state of the health system anymore. It was past that. Now everyone just feared for their lives whenever they left the house.

I was surprised by the number of people at the store. I thought it would just be me.

I walk down an aisle that once had chocolates and snacks.

At the other end appears a woman, maybe in her 40s, pushing a trolley. There's a moment where our eyes meet. Trying to work the other one out. Neither of us wants to move further down the aisle. They want us to keep our distance from one another. Sometimes people will smile at you.

There isn't decomposing flesh like you'd find with the undead. No crosses marked out on their faces. No extra limbs. Or missing limbs. Or thirst for brains. Or blood. Or whatever a mummy wants when it shambles towards you wrapped in its entombing bandages.

You are just presented with a face. Perhaps a face of rage. But you can't assume that someone's features twisted up in a way that the reptilian part of your brain knows mean they want to harm you means that they are infected.

That face could be serene. That face could be vulgar. Beautiful faces. Ugly faces. Faces that look like your friends from primary school.

And you have no idea if this is the person that might infect you.

This isn't the way it's supposed to be. This grocery store is firmly in a middle class suburb. There is an aisle dedicated to gluten free products, as though there are that many with celiacs disease living around here. A section of the store where you can get buckwheat flour, spelt flour, almond flour, garbanzo flour, rice flour, potato flour, hazelnut flour. A guy behind a counter that will slice you fresh sashimi from tuna caught that morning.

Or there would be if people hadn't raided the staples from the store.

This isn't Gorazde. This isn't Adigrat. This is the developed world.

Where civil war happens on the television. Beamed from half a world away. Where we have no fear except of those that look and sound different. It's the others that have to live like this, it's the others that have to live with this.

Maybe an hour's drive from here, where it's all working class and families live pay cheque to pay cheque, wondering whether they have to forego dinner so their kids can eat, wondering if a dental bill or a car accident or losing a job would put them on the street. Maybe there you might expect this.

Now we're terrified of ourselves and soon enough we'll start to turn on ourselves. There's no lever any of us can pull for that.

The moment passes with the woman. Over before it started. Both of us relatively certain that the other one won't lead us to rip our face off in a fit of madness. Both of us cast side eye and keep glancing back at the other as we pass too close for either to be comfortable. There's a sad smile exchanged between us but neither trusts the other.

The shelves have been picked bare. Anything canned is gone. Anything that could be used to cook something has been picked over. Fortunately, the frozen section is still stocked. As though we're on the verge of losing electricity. And maybe we are and maybe I'll look like a fool when it happens. But the kind of meals I eat don't end up on the store shelves. They sit in a freezer waiting for me to microwave them. Filling. Nutritionally complete or near enough to keep me functioning.

The aisle where the toilet paper should be lays bare. A meek sign states a limit of two packs per customer. If you were clever and got here in time to get toilet paper you'd probably form a cartel and make a run on the store to make sure that when the real apocalypse comes you won't have to worry about what you wipe your ass with.

There were always tissues. The store was fully stocked with them. And worst case scenario, when that day came where we'd be eating each other and bathing in each others blood, I wouldn't care if I needed to track which hand I was using to clean myself.

Back home I lost hours to the new hit show. I had overheard them talking about it in the brief moments I had between meetings at work.

Pummelled by Monkeys!

I expect the exclamation is critical to the marketing campaign.

A man walks into an RV. A large one. The sort you could take the extended family in.

A large man. Like his job is sedentary. Like he sits all day staring at a screen. Maybe a lower level bureaucrat. Maybe an office manager type. Probably doesn't like his life much.

In the RV are a bunch of monkeys. Or should they be called apes. Big monkeys. Probably apes. All close enough to be humans that this probably violates some labour code. I don't know. I'm not a regulator.

The monkeys look furious. The monkeys look hungry.

The man isn't ready.

He looks like he doesn't know what to expect when he steps in the RV despite the show being called *Pummelled by Monkeys!*

A monkey grabs him and starts to torque his arm. In the way you would try and get a limb off a mannequin. Yanking at the arm.

Another monkey ambles up and tears the man's face off. Not all of it, skin barely clings to the left side of his face. The right side is a mess. All coagulated blood and muscle. The eye hangs from its socket.

The man screams.

The first monkey tears the arm off.

A carnival style soundtrack plays over the images.

The remainder of the monkeys descend on the man's body (corpse?) and begin to fight amongst themselves over the meat.

Smash cut to a commercial for a deodorising dish washing liquid. I guess they can't doing a coming up next tag before commercial breaks on this show, it would give away the fun.

I use my kitchen sink as a bookshelf these days.

I forgot to buy anything for lunch at the store. You get into a routine where lunch is something that happens during the work day and you don't know what to do when you aren't there. I could eat one of the frozen meals but I plan those for dinner across the week. It's how I afford an apartment like this.

I lose hours to *Pummelled by Monkeys!*

It's late when I decide to check in on the cam girls. I open browser windows with the half a dozen I follow on a regular basis. Three of them aren't online. The other three seem strange.

You can tell a lot by what happens in pornography. Its a key driver of innovation. Innovations we often have to create policy around.

I suggested, in a fit of openness at a Christmas party when The Man, but not the current The Man - The Man two cycles back, visited the offices, that he should think about regulating the cam girl space. Enough that we could pull in some tax dollars from them rather than them plowing it all into costumes for their shows and cryptocurrency, but not so much that we'd stifle the innovation coming out of there. After that I didn't get called up the hill, even as a silent offsider - the sort that passes hastily written notes to the actual servants doing the talking, until the election after and the change of government.

The girls look hollowed out. They're doing what they need to. Sitting there naked. But they aren't doing anything. They don't look like they've slept in days. There is a rage fixed to their faces.

One of the girls looks like she's been cutting. Which isn't completely out of the ordinary for these girls. Having to perform for as long as possible each day to try to get as much eyeballs on themselves, never leaving the same space except when they go on trips overseas but it ends up being much the same and they stay in their hotel rooms most of the trip trying to get more eyeballs on their flesh.

That does something to a person. Any time you have to perform for that long. Any time your livelihood depends on it. Any time you have to spend most of your life presenting yourself as a certain thing, becoming a certain creature. That is going to change the way a person views the world.

One of the three girls that wasn't online blinks into view.

She looks exhausted. She looks manic. Like she's gotten too much sun and is barely staving off passing out.

A dildo repeatedly pushing into herself like her life depends on it. Like she hates herself and is trying to do herself more harm than she ever has.

It will only get worse.

Chapter 36

I needed out of the apartment. The walls felt smaller than I wanted.

It was just supposed to be a starter apartment. Two bedrooms because I thought I would get married and we might need a study or room to do whatever in when we didn't want to be in the others presence. The sort of apartment you get before you have kids. That you can trade up from. That will appreciate in value so once you get to the point where it's time to start a family with that woman you married, you can sell the place and make a cash offer on the family house with 4 bedrooms, 2 bathrooms, an alfresco, and a double garage. Somewhere out in a nice leafy suburb rather than near enough to a university that for half the nights every week you can hear drunk students wandering back to their dorms.

But none of that ever happened and so the second bedroom becomes a place to set up a desk and fill with books and magazines, and it's unlikely that I'll ever sell the place because why would I need more rooms and what would I do with a backyard.

It's moments like this where I long for a backyard or just even a place that doesn't have a toilet in the small laundry room. To not feel like the walls were crowding in on me.

Despite it being winter, the air had been unseasonably warm. Like a fire was always burning somewhere off towards the countryside. I didn't need a jacket if I was going to wander the streets but I might need a knife. Nowhere felt safe anymore. It used to be that I would listen to my podcasts on the walk to the train station each morning. Chatter about policy matters to fill my mornings. Deep dives into how the levers I was pulling were impacting people.

Now, to listen to anything, whether in the morning or at night like this when the light took on a greasy sheen and made everything look somewhat alien, was welcoming disaster.

Outside the building, a man huddled in the entrance near the mailboxes. He looked like a man I'd passed many times, giving the briefest of nods. I wouldn't be able to guess at his name. I couldn't tell you what apartment he lives in. But we both know that we both live in the same building.

Here he was weeping to himself as he huddled into a ball.

There was no way I was going near him. He seemed afflicted. He was probably infectious. In this world, now, if you're foolish, or weak, or try to help, that's when it gets you.

As a cost saving measure due to the drag on the economy from the Shriek, and as a means of trying to get people to stay inside as much as possible, they had started turning off the street lights at night. It made it so you could see the stars.

The cold infinite darkness, enveloping us. Tiny pin pricks of light punched through the dark.

The speckling of stars that you never see unless you get away from the cities.

The vastness of it.

The insignificance of all of us.

In the distance I could hear sirens.

The Shriek seemed to compel people to leave their homes. As though the Shriek felt a need to be near others so it could spread and infect and lead to the ruin of humanity. As though somehow it could survive once we had all torn each other apart.

On the wind was the sound of shouting. Of screams.

Ahead I could see a group of people lit by a fire burning in a barrel. The way you imagine homeless people try to stay warm.

It looked like some sort of fight club. Figures lashing out at one another.

There is a brief flash of a blade in the fire light. And then some of the figures descend on one that had fallen after taking a hit to the face.

I feel hyper aware. It's becoming my normal.

I'm not just aware of what is ahead of me. I'm cautious of any side streets. I am aware of which way my shadow is cast and whether that can tell me of anything coming from behind me or from the sides.

My skin tingles, anticipating something, something from somewhere.

My heart is loud in my ears. I don't feel afraid. Just alert. And clearly my body is taking steps to prepare itself for whatever it believes is coming my way.

I take a wide way around the impromptu fight club. The man that fell to the floor must be dead by now. It looks as though the others are beginning to turn on one another. Menacing shadows being cast on the buildings around them by the fire.

They don't seem to notice me as I slink by in the shadows of the street.

Further down, I pass more people who are weeping. You

never know if it is going to turn into something else, a rage long held down by the need to keep a job or a marriage or out of prison.

Towards the train station, I can see people worshipping at the lesions. More than you normally see during the day. Perhaps this is the new normal. Perhaps more people are beginning to give up what remains of their lives to wait for secrets from the lesions.

Not far from the apartment building there is a large park. The sort of park that spans a few city blocks. Certainly not one of the great city parks of the world but I can find enjoyment walking its path when I have some down time and don't want to be tied to a phone.

There is no fog or anything that gives the air presence but it feels thick, like I am having to actively move through it rather than just walking. I am aware of the air around my skin. A warmth moves past me and I know that I am taking up space amongst the air. Between the air and being in a state of hyper awareness, I feel more alive than I have in years.

I remember when I was in university we used to wander down to the park, drunk or stoned, and just walk the paths. On some nights it felt like you would turn a corner and there would be some unseen horror lurking in front of you because your addled mind and the darkness mingled to create things that weren't there.

Walking into one of the many clearings, pushing past branches as I walk off one of the paths, I see a group of people. Hooded. What little light there is from the night sky casts them in silhouette. It sounds like they are chanting.

I move closer, trying to stick to the shadows.

The chanting seemed to be reaching some sort of crescendo.

Then a woman stepped into the middle of the circle.

The circle had formed around a lesion.

She let the hooded cloak fall from her shoulders so she stood naked.

She raised her hands up to the sky.

Her chest rose up as she took a breath.

"The working is at hand."

The chanting continued.

"Our master is at hand."

The chanting continued.

The hooded people moved closer to her.

"The working is at hand."

The chanting continued.

The hooded people were closer still to her.

"Into the black."

She fell to her knees at the base of the lesion and threw her arms on it.

The hooded people surged towards her as she began to speak in a tongue I did not recognise. There were shreds of possible language leaving her mouth. Words I can barely describe. Despite the heat, the hairs on my arms stood up. The warm breeze dropped.

The hooded people surged as her words got louder and more guttural. Then the hooded people were on her. Hitting her. Wet slapping sounds as she grew bloody. At least one knife punctured her chest. Teeth tore into flesh. The words had stopped. The chanting had stopped. I could hear heavy breathing and a whimper.

Once there was no more life in her body for them to consume, the hooded people scattered into the night. Other worldly strides. Something primal. They let out howls into the night. I thought, for a moment, I heard howls coming from elsewhere in answer but it must surely have been the wind.

Her remains were splashed against the lesion. The lesion looked like it pulsed.

I slunk back into the trees. Looking up through the canopy, the sky seemed horrifyingly large. The world, my existence, a tiny speck meaning, mattering, nothing.

My head felt light.

My veins felt heavy.

My heart beat.

My heart beat.

There was a moment where I swear I could see slices of time reach out in front of me.

A force felt like it was pushing me down into the ground.

Then it was gone and my head was buzzing like a swarm of March flies covered me.

The world was no longer the world I had been born into. I traced my steps back to the apartment building carefully, the sobbing man still in the doorway, and checked four times that I had locked the door to my apartment.

I lay down on the couch and watched *Pummelled by Monkeys!*

A day disappeared as I stared at the screen. Watching a former world that had evaporated when none of us were looking.

I started to cheer for the apes.

Let them tear the skin from the bones of these men hoping they would be the one to survive the RV. Hoping they would be the ones that would finally claim the prize money.

When you have so little, $10,000 seems like a lot.

You could get a mortgage with money like that.

Or a new car.

Or a new phone.

Or could blow it all on whatever it is that caused your brain to flood itself with a happy warm feeling.

I could do with some of that. We all could. At least those of us that weren't faced with our brains stripping themselves out from the inside.

Chapter 37

I awoke and stamped out the campfire in front of me. The fire had kept the darkness at bay as I slept. The cold alien sun from somewhere I couldn't determine was starting to rise.

There was nothing around me. Nothing as far as I could see.

I started walking. I had always been walking. I scratched at the beard that had grown during my time here. My fingernails, blackened with dirt, were longer than they had ever been.

My legs propelled themselves forward. Always walking. Towards what I could not tell.

After a time I could spy the structure again, it gave me direction and purpose.

As I walked I became aware that there did seem to be an edge to this cavernous space. The lesions were thicker here. I needed to carefully make my way through them. They called to me. Sweet infinite whispers.

The edge looked organic. The way you expect the inside of an animal to look. There was something holding it in place that could have been a rib cage.

I put my hand on the edge and closed my eyes. The edge felt warm and wet, like raw meat.

I heard a rumble like movement. My eyes snapped open. There didn't seem to be anything aside from the lesions near me. Had they moved when I wasn't looking.

My hand on the edge, the rumble was in sync with the pulses I felt from the edge.

We moved through the infinite.

I walked towards the structure.

I walked towards the structure.

I walked through aeons.

My hair grew.

My eyes itched.

I slept no more.

Years later I arrived at the structure.

It was cold to the touch. Steam rising where my hand touched it.

The pipes pouring into the structure belched and creaked as some fluid made its way inside.

I peered through the small window at the person sized hatch.

Inside was a man hunched over. Long tendrils attached to him, were part of him, and ran up to the pipes and then disappeared to wherever the pipes went. The man didn't seem to move but the tendrils pulsed like the lesions did when I could look at them.

I watched the man for a day or more, transfixed by his form. He was white in a way that people don't mean when they say something is white. He was the white of chalk. He was the white of the complete absence of darkness.

Then he looked at me and I screamed.

No face. There was no face. No eyes. No mouth. Nothingness. Neverness.

It felt like I was pierced by everything. His head containing a pool of milk that was deeper than anywhere could be on earth. His head containing everything that had been birthed by the universe always.

My skin started to burn.

I screamed.

The scream escaped me. I couldn't make my scream make noise.

I burnt.

I ran.

Chapter 38

The thing you need to understand about Brian is that he works in a public service that isn't much different to the public service that created The End or Geoff. Oh, he might think that it's substantially different. And in some regards he's correct, there isn't such a thing as a typing pool anymore. And it's more likely that women will actually hold positions beyond just being meat to be passed between the men who do the 'real' work. Because the world has moved on since those days and people beyond old white men have rights and get chances.

But the service itself. Well, the service never changes. Not in anyway that actually matters. The systems and processes may change but the work will remain the same.

People always think the service is something that has sprung into being over the past half a century. The administrative state has existed since time immemorial. Ever since there were people in power that needed something done so that the world, or at least their part of the world, had things in place that needed to be in place so their citizens didn't rise up.

Ancient democracies, feudal states, authoritarian regimes, all have had something you could call the public service. It hasn't always been called that but it's always been there. Sometimes respected. Sometimes hated. Most times feared. It has existed.

Because the service, once it came into being, had one goal and one goal only. To grow. To consume. To eat everything around it. To grow fat and bloated. Every conservative politician that has always told their voters that they stand for small government, the service has grown. Because the service grows. The service creates ways of defining its own existence. Of generating projects and policies that will ensure not only its own survival but its growth.

I should know, I worked as a servant for a time. Then I got called up to the hill to work for a politician. I won't tell you which one. Cabinet level but not The Man. I honestly can't think of anything worse than working for The Man. I know people that do, there's an air of smugness that radiates from them and it sickens me. I take comfort in the fact that they are grossly overworked. They think they're the ones that do the real work, the work the servants think they are doing. Thing is, no one is doing the real work, not in government. It's all just noise justifying it's own existence and waiting until the next campaign begins.

Working for one of the Cabinet meant I was in the room when they were discussing the Shriek because I guess that's what we eventually started all calling it. I'm not sure what the moment was when we started calling it that but quickly enough no one wasn't calling it that. Even the medical experts were calling it that come a certain point.

I'm not sure when I decided that I was going to swipe a copy of the Cabinet transcript from that meeting about the Shriek. It wasn't my style. You get in the room, you understand that Chatham House rules are in effect. Those transcripts are marked secret anyway so you just assume that you'll never do anything with them and they'll burst into flame once you've read them. They aren't strictly burn after reading but they're near enough for the sort of information that crosses my desk.

But swipe the transcript I did. It wasn't a big document, and no one noticed given all the documents that I need to stuff in my bag each night when I leave the office because working for a Cabinet level politician means that you are expected to work into the night most nights of the week and if you aren't then it must mean you are out at an event where you're working anyway.

If there was a reason I swiped it, it's because I know that the Shriek can't be a prion. I'm not even sure it's a disease. I don't know what it is, I'm not a scientist, my background is in international relations with a minor in psychology. But I know that Cabinet doesn't know what it is either.

Sure, the early suggestions could have pointed towards a prion. Some fucked up thing that was worming its way into people's brains and sending them so off kilter they were presenting as mental health admissions. Sure, I can see that. But that meeting, the chief medical officer sits there and categorically says it isn't a prion. It's there in the transcript. He doesn't know what it is, that's his quick follow up.

And there's silence. Seven minutes of silence.

Because no one wants to jump in before The Man speaks. The Man looked like he was going to blast the chief medical officer. Just rip the poor man apart just cause The Man got up in front of cameras too quickly and told people something with certainty when he probably should have waited for the science to actually come in with an answer which the science eventually did but it wasn't the answer that The Man wanted to hear. At all. And the chief medical officer could feel all of that, you could see it all over his face. Flop sweat and a scent of fear hanging boldly in the room. No one wanting to catch the eye of anyone else. Like when your father used to come home slightly drunk after a night drinking and you hadn't done your homework or tidied your room and somehow all of that was your mother's fault and you and your siblings just did not know how to react and you certainly weren't going to do anything that might adjust the pressure in the air because that could lead to a scary, terrible outcome that your young brain wouldn't be able to properly understand or process.

Seven minutes. And The Man was just sitting there the whole time, a minute or so in he looks like the initial rage has passed but that just puts everyone more on edge because now everyone is worried that he's become sort of caged animal waiting to pounce.

Seven minutes is a long time at the best of times but especially in a Cabinet meeting. These are busy people, important people, but no one dares mention that because they all know The Man is more important and busier than they. Or at least he should be. Or at least that's how he acts. And the silence keeps going.

Then The Man says that it's a prion and we're telling the people that it's a prion. Says that the chief medical officer said it was a prion and whose to say that the science is right this time because now they're saying it was wrong last time. So now everyone needs to act accordingly. Put in place plans to deal with a prion, come up with vaccines to get rid of the thing, come up with public health measures to stop the spread, start studying this to know what's going to happen to people if this thing isn't contained. All good things. And the chief medical officer breathed a sigh of relief, and then was promptly fired because damn the science if it disagrees with The Man.

You want to know what I think this is? Some super syphilis.

We always forget about syphilis. It's not what it once was but centuries ago it was a killer. And the kicker was before it killed you, it would send you straight up, certifiable insane. Just strip away at your brain and show you all manner of bizarre hallucinations. People used to think the afflicted were possessed by the devil. Because only the devil had a touch that could possibly do that to a person. But then we got antibiotics and now everyone forgets about syphilis but I swear this it, come back again, with a vengeance. Some sort of super version of it that antibiotics won't touch. So now we're all going insane because it's spreading like wildfire. Which would be a good outcome because surely there'd be some scientist somewhere, a university, big pharma, whatever, that could come up with something that kills it stone dead.

But of course, The Man says prion, so the press says prion, so everyone says prion and unless they plan on starting to cook people alive at a thousand degrees Celsius, which even The Man wouldn't think to do or have the stomach for, unless they plan on that then I can't imagine they would be doing anything that would come close to changing this situation. I would know if they planned on cooking people, and I haven't heard anything, at least outside of some darker moments on long nights that we've had in the office where our politician has broken out the scotch a bit earlier than usual. But maybe I'm out of the loop on this one, this one time. It has happened before. Could be the military are out there, circling the skies, waiting to drop pounds of napalm all over us as some sort of cleansing measure. Or better yet, a nuke. Properly wipe all of us fucks off the face of the planet and then hope they can come up with something better next time.

Of course, not everyone I have spoken to believes this is

super syphilis. When I was on my way trying to get out of the city, I came across a kind of hippy commune one evening. I was travelling light, and they seemed welcoming enough, and that maybe I might be able to crash with them for the night. Which is more trusting than I usually am or have learned to become given all of this happening out there.

Anyway, they were convinced that what this had to be, what was causing everything, was the arrival (or return, they sometimes used that word) of some horrific entity from out beyond the stars. Out beyond the edges of the galaxy. All tentacles and weird angles that fold in on themselves. Just came back from some journey spanning aeons. Sitting out there in the Kepler belt, sending bad vibrations that are tearing people's minds apart. The sort of being that to behold would instantly send you into a gibbering mess on the floor, a state from which you'd never return.

I couldn't be sure but it seemed like they were in awe of the thing they believed was out there. Like they were in some sort of worship with it. There was this woman, fairly young, tawny hair, tone body that was with them. I didn't see much of her in my time with the group (which was admittedly, not all that long), as though they kept her from my sight as much as possible. It seemed like she was just babbling randomly whenever I could hear her. But they treated her with such reverence, as though she was an oracle. That granted them divine wisdom. And I would have spent the night with them ultimately, except that one of the men started to turn sinister as night fell. Not touched or afflicted but sinister, as though the group were his harem and with another man around, at least one he hadn't already cowed, there would be some sort of fight for supremacy. I said my goodbyes and headed back out on to the road.

Did you feel that? Just then. I felt like I was about to float away.

These are weird times where travelling can show you how things have frayed, or outright imploded in some towns. I didn't have a specific destination in mind, just that I needed to be away from the city and away from people, especially if this was a super disease, I had no urge to be near people that could infect me.

It wasn't long after those seven minutes of silence when I decided I needed to get out. Sometimes, you get that sense that things are going south and you need to be gone. Some primal part of the brain that runs on instinct and fear and looks like it knows some secret knowledge of the universe before others.

Which meant I was there in those early days when people flocked to the stores and panic bought anything and everything. Never eaten canned beans before, well now you were about to become a connoisseur. You'd just bought two cases of 24 cans a case. I had certainly never baked anything, but now I was the proud owner of multiple large bags of floor. Rice, too.

It wasn't instinct, it wasn't informed by what I could possibly do with any of these things. We were just in a frenzy where we followed each other and didn't have a real sense of anything. Everyone else was buying toilet paper, so it must be a sensible purchase. Everyone was heading for the aisle with powdered and long life milk, so best to load up on those.

Looking at my haul now, at least what is left of it, I can see sense in most of what I purchased. Long lasting goods that won't spoil if the power goes down. *When* the power goes down, speaks that primal part of me. I'll always need toilet paper. I may not enjoy sardines or brined mackerel but they won't go bad on me. So be it. I can ride this out, whatever it ends up being, for months with this haul.

Months from now, when it's all over, we'll look back and chuckle. There will be books, some good, some bad, some that give us insight into how it went wrong and how it went right. Some books will just remind us of how these days felt. We'll all carry stories with us.

This morning, I woke with the sunrise, looking out to the ocean. The sun peaking over the horizon and bathing everything in an early morning glow. The world around me beginning to wake. Nothing around me for miles. I could hear birds in the distance. I felt at peace for the first time in a long time. In forever possibly. My life has always been chaos at the speed of sound. Disconnecting like this. It was perfect. It was all mine. My story from that one day when all this craziness was happening and it was perfect and quiet and still.

But you wanted to know about Brian. When you meet him, there seems to be something missing. You know how a dog will react to people that have something off about them, they'll bear their teeth, that low growl starts, they know danger is present. That's the reaction people have to Brian. He's a strange looking guy, but that's not the reason. Of course, people don't bear their teeth at him. They just seem unsettled and they don't want to meet his eyes.

God, it feels like fire some times.

I'm sure there's enough there to keep people interested if they get past that point. There is with just about everyone in the world, no one is completely repellent to everyone else. I've heard many a reason for why he comes off with that strange air. That he killed his family when he was a young boy. That he killed the family dog when he was a young boy but that never progressed to him becoming some sort of a serial killer or however that sort usually ends up. That he was seeing a therapist from when he was 3 years old because he liked to light fires. That he's heavily medicated. That his parents were killed in a horrific car crash and he was the sole survivor. That his parents are still alive but they got divorced early on and his father, who beat him, got sole custody because his mother was caught up with drugs and ended up selling her body to support her habit. That when he was in high school he was a good student but then this girl got obsessed with him and ended up murdering his then girlfriend and dumping her body in the dumpster at the high school so it was found the next morning and then he had to go through the ordeal of not just a dead girlfriend but also the trial. That he was driving a car one night and he crashed into a pedestrian and nearly, but didn't, kill the guy and ever since he's just been a bit different, a bit haunted.

I've heard all of that. I don't believe any of it. Half the stories about Brian would mean he wouldn't be a servant so much as he'd be in prison or a mental health facility for the remainder of his life. The other half would leave him in a state of near total terror and fear.

The sky looks like latticework.

No. My theory is he's just an asshole. That maybe life didn't turn out the way he wanted and now he's pissed off at the world but professional enough to try and hide that fact but not so good at hiding that fact for people not to notice. Or life just delivered a series of papercuts that all built up over time until he just turned out this way. No life shattering event or events, just little sleights and disappointments. Or he just is kind of shy. Not good at feeling things properly. He isn't a sociopath

162

or a psychopath or any sort of pathy. Just weird.

The public service is home to all sorts. It's got its weirdos. Its cowards. Yes, its sociopaths. But it also has people full of joy with rich lives outside the 9 to 5 drudgery of their job. Scientists. True believers that came to the service because they genuinely wanted to help people. Those that define themselves by their job. Carers. Preachers that have turned their back on the church. Ex-teachers. Musicians. Those that just work there. Writers. Dreamers.

It feels like fire sometimes but I want more of it.

The service of today is so gargantuan that it cannot be a monolith. It is the broadest of churches that will accept anyone that can meet its low bar. Of course there will be those leeching off the tax payer and those that are just using it to climb. But that doesn't mean that is all the service is or can be.

The service grows and sucks more people into its orbit. Forever growing. Forever consuming. Growing. Growing. The service wants to become the monoculture. The service wants to be all there is. I try not to think of the implications and how that would shatter the economy and crowd out the private sector. The service is a beast that has no master. The service is the evolutionary inevitability. It existed long before us and, apocalypse be damned, it will exist long after we're gone. It is an animal, an alien amongst us, that feeds and we will never understand. It will eat all of us eventually, as easily as someone opens up a fridge and pulls out a lunch.

At once the world bursts into flame before my eyes. The flames dance around me. Demons rise from sigils carved into the earth. A whisper touches my ear and then is gone before I can make it out. The demons call to me in a guttural, atavistic language that means nothing and all.

Far on the horizon I see the ghostly outline of a vast monstrosity looking down at humanity from beyond the sky. At once not there but just hiding outside of sight. Large claw like appendages reaching down towards me. Tentacles covering its head like some gorgonic horror. My mind slips away from me.

A shack in the distance. Out overlooking the ocean. I have stuck to the coast most of the journey. Has this been where my journey has lead me. The possibility of restocking some food. The possibility of a weapon. Every other person I have encountered on this journey seems to have been taken in by some odd madness. The Shriek seems to have addled the brains of many but this is a more insidious madness. The madness that denies that there is a crisis at hand. That says it all must be fake. That states, categorically, that the lizard people are behind all of this so they can carry out their masterplan.

The last one I came across went on a bizarre tangent about The Man and how he had been voted into power not by the will of the people but by the elite, whoever they may be. An elite that switched up the real votes and put someone in power that never should have been there. All so they could start their elite plan that all their elite friends had been working on for decades to achieve... something. His endgame was confused, something about climate change being fake but it was real because the elites wanted to reduce the population. Never mind that the elite would be out a workforce so they'd lose production and therefore money. It's best not to engage in too much logic with this sort, I thought. I mainly just nodded. The beer he had, some homebrew concoction, was good so I drank too much and ended up falling asleep with the stars aswirl above.

Come the morning, he was gone, his beer too. Clearly his madness didn't extend to pilfering any of my belongings, they all appeared to be intact when I awoke. I would have happily handed over a can of beans or three if he'd asked but he asked for nothing in return for the beer, just an ear to listen to his story.

It could be that it was another symptom of the Shriek. Seeing things that weren't there, speaking of the whispers that filled ones head. Denying that the end of days was upon us. Worshipping some gigantic horror from outside of space. All just symptoms of a disease that escaped from a lab that wasn't following protocol when doing gain of function research.

The shack looked to be deserted. I checked the floor boards to make sure I wasn't banging around on top of a survival shelter. Last thing I needed was to make myself at home only to find a gun jammed into my cheek while I was carefully preparing a feast of beans and poorly crafted unleavened bread.

As night fell I chanced a fire. It could give away my position to any hostile parties in the area but I wanted to see the flames dancing again. That wild abandon where they consumed the air and rejoiced.

In a cast iron pot, the sort you can never hope to buy from a store anymore, that I found in the cupboards of the shack, I cooked tonight's beans. Alas, the shack had been bare of food or weapons. Either picked clean by those that came before, or never fully stocked to begin with, some sort of fishing shack on the coast that was used for two weeks every year during the season.

The light from the fire blotted out the stars. They had become my favourite part of my journey to nowhere. Forever reminding me of my insignificance and the insignificance of what I chose to do for a living. I imagine that would make many feel small and that they didn't matter.

I found it freeing. It made me feel alive. Faced with my own smallness, my own minuscule nature in an indifferent universe, I realised that my life was worth whatever I did with it. What value I could squeeze out of every day. The wonder that I was allowed to behold. The chances and coincidences that had to pile up for my life to have ever happened. I screamed into the night. A scream of joy. Of casting off my skin. Of becoming one with it all.

My insides crackled with potential. I needed more of it. I needed to feel this forever without life getting in the way. I felt high and alert. I felt my edges starting to bleed outside my form.

Through the flames, outside the edge of the light, a woman came into focus. Lithe would be the word poets would use. Small footfalls that I couldn't hear above the crackle of the flame. Her eyes crinkled as she smiled. She reminded me of the girl I had been dating back in the city, that I had not called since I hit the road and ran out of phone battery.

Confidently she walked towards the fire. She stopped about a metre from the fire, the opposite side from me so that I had to watch her through the flames. She started to move on the spot. A slow dance, a rhythm I could not place. Seductive. Inviting. Limbs moving fluidly into the night. She looked happy. The flames danced looks of nightmare on her face sometimes. Light and shadow painting the infinite of potential faces.

After a time, minutes, hours, most of my life, I slowly stood and made my way around the fire to her. She did not hesitate or move back as people so often do these days or even stop her movement. I offered my hand to her, in lieu of grabbing her as

I wanted.

She took my hand and pulled herself in close to me. Our hips pressing together. Her movement not ending. We danced. We danced. We danced. Both absorbing the other's rhythm and making it our own together.

I rested my head on her shoulder and lightly kissed her shoulder. Still our movement continued. We were becoming as one. More sensual than I had ever experienced. We were discovering the other halves of ourselves.

Slowly, almost imperceptibly, we began to dissolve to the ground. Becoming as dust. Falling. Falling. Dissolving together, to join the infinite.

As I fell I saw something outside the edge of reality. A colour that I would never be able to name, that I had never seen. A thing. Giant. Horrific. All consuming. Come to eat all of us with its great maw and tentacled appearance. Devouring stars like I had once eaten cereal. That had come for us now after all these aeons. That would consume us and would never realise what it had taken from the universe because it was not of this universe.

My mind shattered.

I smiled.

I laughed.

My ears filled with a roar that I would always hear from now until forever was over.

The woman. My perfect spectral woman was with me. We would never be apart. I was her. She was all that I was.

The cast iron pot had heated. The beans had started to boil. Would continue to boil until the fire died down in the early hours of the morning. The beans would turn. Ruined. A man and his dog, tired from walking after their car had broken down two days before, would come across the remnants a week later.

Waves on the beach crashed below the cliff on which stood the shack. The shack's owner would never return for a fishing season, caught up in a riot half a world away whilst travelling for business. Screams and shouts from those afflicted surrounding him as he clutched at his head as a Shriek struck.

The stars were silent.

The breeze blew, unseasonably warm for this time of the year at this point on the coast.

Chapter 39

It felt safe in the office. My little refuge from the world where I understood the rules and there was little that could cause me to despair.

James had beaten me into the office. There he was sitting at his desk. Screen on. Emails to get through. The coffee in his hand looked mostly finished.

I'd spent too much time watching the people worship the lesion out the front of the train station. I'd begun to wonder if they were seeing something that I wasn't. As though it did not appear as some cancerous growth. Perhaps it appeared an angelic creature, a siren calling to them and rooting them in place. I wasn't hearing the calls they were. Just the whisper. *Into the black*. Maybe they heard the same. Maybe we were hearing the same voice coming from some psychic limb buried deep in our minds.

"You'll need to see what they sent back down from the hill on the child care subsidy," which was as much as a 'hello' as James and I often threw to one another when we saw each other after time apart.

Of course the email about it was flagged high importance. Of course the agency head and deputy head had spent the past 24 hours piling on the email thread about it.

My eyes widened as I read through the marked up submission we had sent up the hill. I shouldn't expect much else after this long. We might be the ones that work out the words for our lords and masters but they often tell us the words that we have to work out.

"But this will mean…" and I wasn't sure what to say beyond that. James and I both knew what this meant but to say it out loud would bring it crashing into reality.

"Yep. They want to get rid of the subsidy."

"So women's participation is just done? That's what we're talking about now?"

"Unless you think that this is a radical repositioning of the family unit in modern society and they're going to follow it up with some massive tax funded whatever that will mean that young fathers are going to start raising their kids, that's what this means."

"But. But they're the liberals. Did I miss an election cycle? The ones that spend big and grow the social welfare state. Right? Did I take two days off and The Man has changed? Who is The Man right now, right now, James?"

"The same The Man it was 2 days ago and an election cycle ago. He's always been fiscally conservative, you know that. I don't know what this is. The End came by last night before I went home and was muttering about reshuffles and portfolios changing hands. Maybe it's part of that. Maybe The Man has the Shriek."

I'd never considered The Man getting the Shriek. Politicians need to be down to earth enough that voters think they aren't some grinning maniac that would eat their children and burn their house to the ground but in the service they become something like gods. Sitting on their mountain top, decrees slipping from their perfect mouths.

A politician doesn't get a disease. A politician doesn't need sleep. A politician doesn't exist in this realm.

But if The Man got the Shriek. What then? How would anything work?

Would those decrees become twisted commands that order us to go out and wipe anything Other from the face of the planet. Would all the power plants be ordered to full output in the hopes that the world would choke. Would they extinguish the service? Would we be subjected to ritual sacrifice to decide elections now, entrails auguring each new era of government.

My arms looked scratch. Like I'd lightly cut them at some point while watching *Pummelled by Monkeys!*

"We need to have a meeting. Like now. I don't want Geoff across this, not yet, but we'll need something because he'll be prowling around to fire at someone on this."

"He came by yesterday, not long after The End."

"Ben! Ben! Where the fuck is Ben?"

James pointed towards a Ben shaped hole in the window that I hadn't noticed when I sat down.

There it was, next to the Terry shaped hole. There were other people shaped holes across the face of the window.

There were less people than normal when I looked across the floor. James and I would often be part of a handful of people in the office early but by now I would expect people to be filtering in.

"It's not just Ben is it?"

James' head made a jerking, twitching movement for a second.

"More and more people aren't coming in. It's not like that's much different to how it is in the real world. This feels like the end of the world, Brian. That's how people are acting. Have you looked at the sort of things people are saying online. All the conspiracy stuff. That this is manufactured. That it's not a disease. That it's a way to subjugate the people. This isn't just the lunatics anymore, this is normal people. There was a friend of mine from like a decade ago, I was on social media this morning and he was on some major rant about how The Man is working with The Queen to wipe out half the world's population so that the climate can recover. One of my granddaughters, my own flesh and blood, was telling me on the phone that the disease is real but it's been weaponised because once you have it they, she never said who 'they' are but there was a tone in her voice suggesting that I was part of 'they', so that they can mind control people to do their bidding. I don't know where this is coming from but it's sent people to a strange place. They never should have given us the internet. Even if this was a real disease to start with, it's become something more like mass hysteria now. Have you seen the people outside the train station down there? Just in a trance in front of those, those things. I don't even know what to call them. Sooner or later, people are just going to stop coming in. And we might never know what happens to them. If they jump like Ben and Terry then sure, we can say we know but what about others? They just don't turn up and we have no idea whether they've done something like jump or are just taking time off away from this madness."

"Okay, who's here then? Derrick? Sarah? Get them in to a room, just book whatever. I don't think we need a screen or a phone or anything but we need to get in a room and work through everything they've sent down from the hill. All that other stuff, I don't know what I can and I can't think about it right now, we just need to keep working. There will be an end to whatever all of this is, and if we stop doing the work now then once we hit recovery we won't have anything to kick start things."

"Sure," James said but I knew he didn't believe me.

Chapter 40

His god was a mad god. His god was a generous god.

He stood in the shadows. Watching the well-suited man as he crept through the street. The people were afraid.

The smell of smoke thick in the air.

The well-suited man held a gun in his hand. He saw the man's hand shaking.

The well-suited man fell to his knees and gripped his head. A moan travelling on the night air.

Further down the street he saw a pack of people. Hollering into the night. Knives. Guns. Fire. Rage on their faces, weapons in their hands.

He waited. He watched. This was what he did.

His mad god had forsaken him. He was immune. When those people would clutch at themselves and moan and have their faces warp, he felt nothing.

There was no change for him. He had always felt this way.

He did not know why his generous god had forsaken him in this way.

The well-suited man had spotted the pack heading his way. Ducked into the threshold of a door. Hoping he would be kept safe by the darkness.

He came out of his shadow and moved silently across the

street to near the man. The pack moved loudly down the street. They passed without incident. Their shouts echoing back towards him. Screams were heard from the night.

The man looked to see if the pack was far enough gone that he could come out of his hiding place. He glanced around, then started on the route he had been following before.

Sliding out of the shadows, he followed the well-suited man.

His mad god had forsaken him but his was a generous god.

He walked softly behind the man. His steps lengthening to slowly gain on his prey. His foot crunched too loudly on a broken brick.

The well-suited man stopped. He looked around. Furtive in his movements. The man didn't see him and started to move.

He was close. He got closer. People chose knives. They chose guns. They thought those things would keep them safe from his mad god.

Longer steps. Longer steps.

He was upon the well-suited man. He pushed him to the ground. The gun fired. A bullet streaking up into the night. Just another sound in the limitless noise.

He felt a warmth. He felt an itch. His face felt stretched.

The well-suited man groaned. Face down. Back inviting.

He jumped on the man's back. He squeezed his hands around the neck. Tighter. Tighter. He felt a spinal pop between his hands. He squeezed.

The man thrashed. The gun fired again. Hitting a wall nearby.

The well-suited man went limp.

His god was a mad god. He would wash the streets in blood and his mad god would return to claim him.

Chapter 41

"I just don't understand why you care. You don't even have kids," which was as good a way of Derrick saying he didn't want to have this meeting. Which made sense, I could understand the position of not wanting to do the work if this was the actual end of days. But that was our role.

"You're better than that, Derrick. You don't want to do the work, then just say as much. Otherwise we can play rhetorical nonsense all day. I don't have a wife either, so I guess I shouldn't care about rape victims? How about the fact that I don't have an adopted Chinese son, so I probably shouldn't give a fuck about sweatshop labour? Or maybe we go out and start slaughtering dogs and cats because I don't have either of those."

"I don't want to work on this. I don't see the point. They've sent it back down from the hill with their changes, you know how the game is played. We accept those and rework things so it works for the politicians. That's how it's always been."

"I know. But this is just, it's just beyond a line, you know? In this day and age to try and pull this stunt. I don't know if it's because of the election. Maybe it's the Shriek. Maybe The Man's wife isn't putting out. Whatever it is, it's too much. We have years and years of modelling that says if you make child care free, women's participation skyrockets and the policy will pay for itself. This is the opposite. It's going to be a drag on productivity which will be a drag on the greater economy. Which…"

"Yes, Brian. We all know that. But that's not what we do is it? We give them options, whether they dictate them to us or not, then they choose. Not us."

Back in university, they teach you that as a policymaker if you run into a situation that you cannot stomach morally, then you have to resign. That is what a good policymaker does. You don't sabotage policy. You use your position to send a signal that the Government is doing the wrong thing, then hope they care you resigned. Of course, in university, they don't teach you that your resignation only matters if you're a high level bureaucrat. That if you're just some random mid level servant then no one cares. So there is no point in resigning. And it's only those high level servants that can actually afford to resign like that, and they'll be snapped up within minutes of their resignation being accepted. Usually by the board of some major corporation or bank, the sort of seat that at my level you never imagine will happen.

"Have you got anything, James?"

"Derrick is right, and you know he's right. I'm as shocked as anyone by this change in policy setting but Derrick is right. I can't see how we change this. In fact, I think there will be a number of people across the agency that applaud this change."

Geoff would probably be one of them.

"Well, I, for one, think it is an excellent change," stated Sarah. There was always something rather uncomfortable when someone in the office made their political views known. Or maybe it was just when those views ran conservative.

Like that time you found out that Claire hated immigrants.

This mostly sweet, nearing retirement woman that you'd only seen get worked up about her grandson telling her he was an atheist, spewing out vile xenophobia.

Silence hung for a moment. The rest of us didn't know what to say to that.

"This means that mother's can stay at home and make sure their children are safe. That no one can get to them. You know there are all sorts of cultists out there that sacrifice children. It's for adrenchrome. The rich run the cults and send them out to kidnap children so they can be tortured and sacrificed."

The words ran from her mouth. She was left panting. Her chest heaved. Sweat rolled down her brow.

No one knew what to say. I considered asking if she'd finished the briefing note.

I felt light headed. I have no issues with managing people that disagree with me, I think that can be useful. This was something else. This was something darker.

I looked at James and Derrick.

"James, Derrick, can you give me and Sarah a moment?"

They shuffled out, not knowing where to look but clearly relieved that they would be away from whatever Sarah was going through.

This must be the Shriek at work. I hadn't seen it close up. Which is one of the advantages of not having real ties to the real world.

"Sarah, look, are you okay? Do you want to just sit in here and take a breath? We can go back out to the floor when you're..."

"You motherfucker! Why did you send them away? Charlie wouldn't have done that. Charlie was a real leader. He knew what to do." Her voice was becoming guttural.

"Fuck you. Fuck you. Fuck you." The last one came out as something like a roar.

I flinched.

"They're killing the children. I have seen it. They are eating them." She started to pull at her skin like it was fitting too tight.

"You are killing them. Fuck you Brian. Sitting in front of your computer doing nothing. All day doing nothing. Brian doing nothing. Fuck you. It's people like you that make me sick. You're a fucking traitor. I hope you rot away in some prison some day. Because there will be a day of reckoning. Can't you feel that it's here. It's now. This is when he comes back and descends and will obliterate all of you sinners."

Tears streamed down her face.

I didn't know what to do.

I quietly left the room and left her to whatever twisting of her mind was happening. We couldn't lock the doors but I could make sure I had meetings for the rest of the day until she left.

I felt hungry.

Chapter 42

I needed out. The Shriek had withered the number of servants that I could arrange a meeting with. Regardless, I needed to be away from all of this for a time. The perks of being in charge meant no one would question my not being around. They would probably rejoice.

I brought James up to speed on the situation with Sarah. James was hardly the action hero but he barely flinched when I told him the state she was in when I left the room.

If she was to come tearing out of the room in some sort of blood frenzy, or if she came out and wept at her desk for the rest of the day, there was nothing I could expect James to do. It's not like he was going to subdue her, you can't ask a servant to go outside of their job description. But best that someone was across the situation.

I felt calm but there was something overwhelming about the encounter. Like a primal force that was speaking through people now.

James listened and then turned back to his emails. As I wandered away from his desk he mentioned that HR was interviewing people. Apparently someone kept stealing lunches from the break room.

I searched for a quiet room. Far enough from the team

that the chances they would stumble across me was severely reduced.

What I was looking for presented itself on the 22nd floor. Similar to the situation on 23, there were less people than usual. I had my pick of the quiet rooms. The one with the comfy chairs that sit across from a conference phone was the ticket. No one could ever get work done in here. The lighting was all wrong. The seats too low. It was good for having a coffee or a nap.

Sliding the door to the room closed behind me, my body wanted to collapse. Finally a moment to relax and be away from it all.

My shoulders heaved as though I was sobbing but no tears came from my eyes.

I stood there. Staring at the wallpaper in the room. The dim lighting masking how hideous it was, designed by a committee of blind monkeys. Browns and brown-golds. Flecks to give the appearance of class.

I kept staring. My eyes started to see beyond the pattern. The wallpaper looking like it breathed. My pulse in sync with whatever creature was living behind the wall.

I stood in place for hours. Thoughts going to the team. Thoughts going to the world outside. No single thought interesting enough to properly turn over in my head. There would need to be significant messaging campaign for the change on the subsidy. We wouldn't have the budget for it. The Man wouldn't accept being the one that had to sell this to the public. It would be communicated that this was an agency decision, the politicians couldn't be held responsible for the impact this would have on people.

Sweat dripped from me. It was too hot in this room. The

fires were everywhere now, started by the afflicted. Any air conditioning struggling to cope with the fumes being pumped into the sky.

A red haze refracted through the glass of the sliding door. The sun was starting to set. The 23rd floor called me back, even if just for a moment to collect my things and fight my way back to my apartment. The train station was slow to move through now with all the people fixed in worship of the lesions.

Hopefully the Sarah situation had been resolved.

Chapter 43

I couldn't hear anything coming from the room where Sarah had been. The door was shut.

James sat staring at his computer. It wasn't that out of the ordinary to see him in this position towards the end of the day. It was the stereotypical servant pose to look like one was deeply contemplating something of great importance to cover for the fact that they either had run out of work or simply didn't want to do what was on their plate.

I couldn't tell you what it was that I saw that made me feel as though this wasn't the normal, killing off the last half an hour of the work day pose. I'm not sure there even was something that could be seen by the eye that lead me to that conclusion. Or maybe it was everything that could be seen with the naked eye but all of that everything was just slightly where it shouldn't be. Almost as though you were looking at someone entirely different despite how their face looked.

I opened with a simple, "Derrick gone?"

And a simple nod is what I received in return.

But it was a slightly slow nod.

"What happened with Sarah?"

"She... security came and took her away."

He wasn't moving. The words came out of his mouth heavy

but quiet. Like it was difficult for him to speak.

"Did anything more happen after I left?"

He nodded, "She got louder and louder and started to bang against the glass. Looks like that stuff is thicker than we give it credit for. I called security. They came up and got her. She managed to get one of them with a good hit before they got her to the ground."

"You seem... I don't know... it there something wrong?"

"Everything is fine, Brian. Everything is fine. Everything is fine. I've seen something."

"To do with Sarah? What did you see?"

"Not Sarah. Something else."

"Come on, James. Come on. What?"

"You know how the elevators have been running slow since all this started?"

"Well, rather than deal with the elevators, I decided to use the stairs. You ever count the stairs in there? 700 from here to ground. So I walk into the stairwell. I swear when I opened the door the lights were on but as I walk through the door, they cut out. It didn't go to darkness that I couldn't see in. It was more like a grey to everything in there. Almost like when your eyes adjust to darkness but it happened straight away. The emergency lights didn't seem to come on like you'd expect them to if the power went out.

"So I started walking down. I think I'm making good time. I was timing myself, glancing at my watch every once in awhile, just to make sure that in the end this could be a quicker way than waiting on those elevators each day, you know.

"The stairs seemed normal enough at first. Then they started to feel wrong. Not wrong, maybe that's the wrong word. Like they were moving me strangely. In the wrong direction. I knew my feet were moving forward and moving down. I could see they were doing exactly that. But to my head it felt like they were going sideways and travelling me somewhere that I didn't mean to get to.

"Those emergency shelters they have every floor, where people in wheelchairs can stop when there's a fire, or a fire drill. I've never understood how those help. Those shelters. One of them wasn't that little alcove in the wall. It opened into a hallway. I'd never seen that there before. Not that I spend a lot of time in the stairwell but it seemed out of the ordinary. So I walked into the hallway.

"The light was different in there. It made me feel ill. This sort of green that reminded me of vomit, or my mother's pea and ham soup, or an ooze that you'd spread on your gums to fight tartar. The hallway was longer than I could possibly imagine this building could house. It felt like I walked it for so long that I'd have to be on the other side of the river. There were doors on either side of the hall but they weren't actual doors. They were like a child's drawing of a door. From when a child is only a few years old. Some sort of chalk paint.

"And then the hallway just ended. There was nothing down there. No door. Not even one of the badly drawn doors. I turned around because I figured I'd have to go back. I didn't feel bad or scared there. But I needed to go back because we only get so long on lunch, you know.

"When I go back out of the hallway and I was in the stairwell again, I looked up and I swear, I swear Brian, that I was looking down towards the ground. I couldn't see that far down or up or whatever way I was looking but something just told me that I wasn't looking up like I thought I was trying to with my head. And I kept moving my feet. It kept feeling every flight or so that gravity was shifting. That's the best way I can describe it. One step I'd be moving down, I knew I was moving down. The next step it felt as though I was going up. It didn't matter that I could see that my feet were moving forward and down. That didn't matter. My head was telling me something else entirely.

"I started to notice that the stairs were almost folding in on each other. The look of them, I mean. The way that you would walk from one step but it kind of looked like the next step was part of the step that you had come from. It was starting to get colder. More than my head not knowing which way was up or which way I was moving, that thing with the steps got to me. You know what I mean when I say that, like it set off something deep in me, in my gut.

"But then the light started to dim. It was ever so slow. Just barely perceptible. I didn't even notice for awhile. It's not like it was bright to begin with. Then at one point it tipped from my being able to see to my eyes grasping, that's not the right word for it but I'm sure you know what I mean, to see anything. Straining, that's probably the word I'm looking for. Until finally, I couldn't see anything. It was complete darkness. But I kept walking. Whatever was happening, there would have to be an end and if I just stopped I worried that maybe it would never stop being dark again.

"I hadn't checked my watch in awhile, so I looked down but I couldn't see it at all. Even when I hit this button here on the side, see this here, that illuminates the face of the watch. See, I know we're under lights right now but you can see how it lights up. It's pretty bright, especially if you're somewhere very dark. But the button didn't do anything. It was like the darkness wasn't the absence of light so much as it was actively killing off any light.

"Eventually, I could see something ahead of me. It felt like I'd stopped walking on stairs. As I got closer to the something, I could see that around it was darkness but the thing itself was quite bright. It seemed to exist in an endless plane of darkness.

"It seemed like frost was everywhere. From whatever light it looked like ice hung in the air.

"When I got within maybe 20 metres of the thing, I could see that it was a person. A man, more to the point. He was naked and hunched over and white in a way that you wouldn't use to describe an actual human being. He was white in the way chalk is white, or white paint is white. Actual white. He looked rough around the edges, as though he was almost painted on to the darkness. How those doors had looked, that was kind of how he looked. But those doors had been obviously fake and not there, just drawings, but this man was actually there. Hunched over, almost like he was in some sort of fetal position, or what's that yoga thing? Child's pose?

"There were tendrils that came from all over him. They were the same colour as he was and they just stretched out into the darkness around him. You couldn't see them once they were out in the darkness. They slightly pulsated. It was like they were some sort of umbilical cords that did something, fed him, kept him alive. I'm not sure, it was hard to tell what I was looking at.

"He didn't move as I approached him. He didn't do anything while I was there near him. I could hear him muttering or babbling as I was walking towards him. I probably heard that noise before I could actually see him, I just didn't realise at the time that it was coming from someone rather than something or somewhere.

"And when I got close enough I could hear him, 'What do

you regret?'

"I had no idea if he was speaking to me or it was just words that bubbled up out of his muttering. I didn't say anything in reply to him. Just kept on staring because I just didn't know what else to do or if I should leave or speak to him or ask him if he needed help.

"He let out a low moan, you know when you hear an elephant roar out in pain, it was a sound like that but quieter. And this image, or I think it was an image, maybe it was an actual thing, anyway, this image of a woman came out of the darkness and walked towards him. She moved slowly, I guess that's why I thought it was an image, something about her and how she moved reminded me of a movie projector. She was wearing old clothing. The clothing was the sort of thing you'd see in those photographs from the Victorian era, you might not have seen many of those but I'm sure you know what I mean, from around the time that cameras were first around. High necked, lots of lace, long skirt that practically dragged across the ground, not that I could tell where there was ground or if there was even ground.

"As she got closer to the man, I could see that it was my maternal grandmother. Much younger than I had ever seen her. Maybe the sort of age she had been when she met my grandfather. She must have died when I was a teenager. We lived out in the country back then, I don't think my mother heard she had died until a few days later. At the time we'd called her senile but looking back it was probably something like dementia or Alzheimer's, I don't think we knew about that back then or certainly it wasn't something I remember my parents saying. I'd stopped visiting her once I got to high school. It was too hard to visit her, she could barely make

188

words and when she could it was all things where she was confused and couldn't remember straight.

"When she got close enough to the man, she looked over towards me. I don't know if she could actually see me or not but her eyes were looking straight into mine. And then, she just sort of crumbled. Like whatever she was, an image or something tangible, whatever it was, just sort of turned to dust and fell towards the dark. Then she was gone.

"In that moment where she turned to dust, I felt something like a heart attack. I could feel it in my arm and my chest, that's why I thought 'this is a heart attack and you're dying.' I started to breathe heavy, it didn't feel like I was doing it, almost a compulsion. And I cried, Brian, I cried and they were heavy tears that disappeared into the darkness below. And the man, he didn't move but his mutters became words again and he asked, 'What do you wish for from your life?'

"After what happened with my grandmother, I fully expected that some ghostly apparition of my wife that passed would appear in the same way. My body was even prepared for it. My heart started to pounded in my chest. Blood thumping in my ears. I wanted to get away but I wanted to wait and see her face again, I wanted that so much. And then... nothing. There was some sort of glimmer out in the distance, a rustle of light, but she never appeared. Nothing ever appeared. And I waited, and I watched the man with his muttering and his umbilical cords pulsing out into the dark, and I waited.

"And I waited. I don't know how long I waited. And watched. But I wanted something more, I wanted some sort of a vision. Again. Like he had given me. Or however that had happened. But he just kept muttering. So I started to move closer to him, to see if I could get him to do it again.

"I'll admit, I worried at one point that if I got too close to him, that if I entered that sphere of light he was giving off that maybe I would turn to dust and just fade away into the nothing. But I was fine with that, or at least fine enough to keep going towards him.

"The light didn't seem to do anything to me but I noticed that I could see more of myself than I had been able to before I approached him. I got right up to him. He didn't move or turn towards me, just that low babbling that he kept making. I stopped for a moment and tried to see if I could make out what he was saying but it was just nonsense. It wasn't even words, or maybe it was but he was saying them too fast. It just sounded like tones, like a child might make when they can't speak yet, or how my grandmother sounded the last time I can remember seeing her.

"I crouched down and moved around to his head. I wanted to make sure that if I was speaking to him that I could see if he was hearing me at all. I noticed that the umbilical cord things were part of him. They weren't tubes or anything like that. It was just smooth skin that reached out from him into the darkness. Dozens of the things, all eating for him or something close enough to that. I guess 'skin' is the best word for it. He looked something more than real up close. Like looking at him was hard because he was so just there, I know that doesn't make any sense when I say it out loud. He just existed more than anything I've ever seen. Looking at you now, I know you exist and you're here and you're real but he was that and more so.

"When I got to his head, I asked him, 'Are you okay? Do you need help?'

"It's not what I wanted to know but that roar from earlier

made me think maybe he was in some sort of pain or he wasn't here because he wanted to be.

"He just kept muttering. Muttering. Muttering. Muttering. Babbling. Muttering. Just this constant noise. There was a rhythm to it, almost a beat. It felt like it was getting louder and louder in my head and it just wouldn't stop. Wouldn't end.

"Then he looked up at me and there was nothing there. No eyes. No mouth. Nothing. Just endless nothing. It was like I was staring into the heart of the universe. The heart of everything. And there was nothing there. But despite all the nothing, there was a flash in my mind of a gaping maw, sharp teeth.

"And then I ran. I ran from it all. Back into the darkness. It seemed like most of my life to get back to that part where the grey had been but when I got there it seemed more like the regular stairwell. It seemed like far more than 700 steps. It seemed like the building must be a thousand stories high with all the stairs there were but I kept going, pushing myself to get up the stairs, until finally, I collapsed against the door to the 23rd floor. My heart felt like it was going to pound its way out of my chest, so I waited until that calmed down and I walked back in here and sat down at my desk. I'm not sure that I've moved since."

When someone tells you they've had what is clearly a psychotic break and seen hallucinations on a grand scale, what can you say to that?

The air felt cold in the office. And James still hadn't moved. His face didn't betray any emotion now. He had told me a tale, a fantasy, a symptom of the Shriek for sure. His brain stem beginning to strip itself until he would be a gibbering mess.

"I think, you need to go home, James. Call it a day. Just rest.

If you don't feel up to tomorrow, then just take the day off. Take a few. You're obviously dealing with something," was the best I could muster up. If we needed to do the work at the moment then James would be no good to us, even if we were down to three of us in the team now.

"I'm leaving, Brian," he replied.

"Good. Just, look, take it easy. And keep me posted on how you're getting on. Yeah?"

"No, Brian. I'm leaving. I'm done with all of this. Don't worry, I'm not about to throw myself out the window like Terry or Ben did. I'm just leaving, all of this. I'm done with being a servant. I don't know what I'm going to do now. I can work that out later. But this, I'm not doing any of this any more. Not after today. Not after that. None of this matters. If nothing else, that's what I learnt from that thing down there. None of this matters. You have to see that. We keep coming here and we achieve what? When was the last time we did anything that achieved something or that we felt good about doing? I'm leaving, Brian."

James picked up his bag and then walked off to the elevators. I thought of running after him. Catching him as he walked on to the elevator. I would have time. Even if I gave him a 5 minute head start I'd still find him waiting at the elevator for another 10 before it arrived.

I thought of begging him to stay. I thought of what the office would be like to come in tomorrow morning to find his desk empty. His computer switched off. The banter not happening while my machine started up and my coffee cooled.

Chapter 44

Each Shriek felt different. Some gave visions. I had those most often when I was asleep. Some made me thirsty for something that I knew I would never taste. Some felt like insects crawling under my skin. Some reminded me of the words 'sickle cell disease' and made me feel as though my veins were being ripped apart by some microscopic organism deep inside me.

I was taking all the precautions I could think of, the mandated and the common sense. Not standing near people. I had started to wear a mask, it made the few meetings with the few people left difficult. Not touching things that I wasn't going to take home with me and boil clean. I had considered wearing surgical gloves but I thought that might be a step too far and make me look insane but then I thought that the world was clearly insane around me so how I looked probably wasn't of concern anymore.

Some of them left me with migraines where I had to clumsily compose emails to let someone at work know I would be in late so I could stay inside with the blinds closed and darkness enveloping me.

Some made me feel the urge to open all the blinds and look down towards the street level and try and find the nearest fire that had been sparked by one of those gripped by the latter stages of the Shriek. I'd stare for hours. Transfixed by the flame dancing around in the sweltering air.

Some made me think that being as hollow as I was or had become or had always been meant that whatever the Shriek tried to do to a person's brain, or managed to do, didn't work on me because there was nothing there for it to strip away at.

When I trudged out of the train station now, the lesions were gone. The crowds still swarmed in places where the lesions had been. I would struggle to peer through the people to see what they surrounded. A beautiful woman stood in the centre of the people. Long golden hair. An aura that seemed to extend far beyond her body. Ethereal. Not quite there. A person etched on to the fabric of reality. She smiled beatifically at the people that surrounded her.

People stretching out to touch the diaphanous dress she wore. They wept as their finger tips brushed against it.

Beckoning me to join them as she stretched out her. I would shyly shake my head and smile as warmth filled me.

Some days, when I would see one of the few people still left on the floor at the office clutching at their head and moaning in clear pain, when they were doing that and I was feeling nothing, despite the fact that the Shriek always seemed to be simultaneously for everyone, at those times I would think maybe I was immune, that maybe if some scientist could harvest my red cells or white cells or whatever they would need that maybe they could come up with some sort of vaccine for all of this, that my blood could heal this world gone mad.

A few minutes later another Shriek would strike and I would feel like I had gone blind for a minute and I knew there was nothing special about my blood or my flesh and that eventually, one day, maybe after everyone else in the world but one day, I would succumb.

Charlie was still around.

Derrick was still around.

I could sense The End but I hadn't seen him in days.

If ever there were two servants with as little going on in their lives as I did, it was them. Derrick may have had kids but they didn't seem to provide much of a life for him. I suspected he was a terrible, or at least absent, father. The Shriek showed the truth of us all.

I tried to concentrate on the emails waiting for me. People were sending them at odd hours of the night. People often did in times of crisis. Can't sleep, need something to distract them from the chaos.

The insane and the desperate rarely take a moment to proofread their emails before hitting send.

There was a request from HR to meet for an interview regarding the lunch thefts. It didn't strike me as anything that should be a high priority but given the lack of staff, it was probably the thing keeping the HR advisers focused enough to not jump or worse.

No one has ever been fired for stealing anyone's lunch ever. That was unlikely to change, especially given the current diminished staff population. But if it kept them away from the real work then it was probably for the best.

Derrick sauntered in around 10am. We were all keeping odd hours. He looked gaunt. Haunted. Infected. I had a sense of those that were about to turn by now. The momentary shifting features. Face skin pulled tight as though they were about to bare their teeth. A smile that looked like it would eventually split their face. The relentless itch. They could never stay still, not even for a moment. Most ended up lightly scratching at their skin. And their smile got wider.

Derrick had some of the signs. Not all. Enough of them to make me keep my distance.

"What have they got us doing today?" he asked, smile too false.

"Something about protective gear. You know, face shields, masks, that sort of thing. Sort of thing they think might slow things."

"We going to be making them? You got a sewing machine tucked away in a quiet room or something?"

I laughed. It wasn't particularly funny but a wave of relief passed over me and I could see some of Derrick. Perhaps I had misread him when he came in. Perhaps he wasn't infected. Perhaps he was destined to be the one left to turn the lights off on the world.

I needed more sleep than I was getting. I hadn't been eating enough. My mind felt sluggish. I felt strangely at ease.

"Yeah, we're going to start a side hustle manufacturing all the protective gear anyone could ever need. Right from this office. We'll put up a sign and everything. You cut. I'll sew. I'm sure we can find something for Charlie to do, he's still around."

"And don't forget The End, he's still around, haunting the halls. Maybe put him on distribution strategy or something. He was always good with logistics."

"Yeah, and the agency head and deputy, they can be marketing. We'll make a mint."

And we laughed. And it felt good. I hadn't felt this good in a long time. My skin felt alive. I could feel the air around me. My head felt clear. And we kept laughing. It was loud. It came from deep in me. I never wanted to stop laughing.

"You think that maybe the reason we haven't been infected is that there's nothing to infect?" I asked.

He smiled that friendly smile, "Could be. Could be. I thought last night that maybe I was immune. Chances are I'm not. No one ever is, not really. That sort of thing happens to people you hear about, not yourself."

"I was thinking that maybe because we're so hollow that we have almost a superpower against the disease."

"It's not a disease."

And I believed him.

"So it not a disease, then what?"

"You know what this is. You know. We all do. This is God. It's his wrath."

"I always took you for an atheist."

"Oh, I am. Or was. I don't know. But this, I mean, this is... I genuinely don't know what else this could be. This isn't a disease. It has to be that we have lived lives that angered the Lord. Now he's come and struck us down with the mother of all plagues. God is the Old Testament God and he is fucking furious."

And we laughed.

And we laughed.

I looked up, past Derrick. I noticed that we were the only ones on the floor. There was a bend at the end of the floor and I wondered if there was anyone down there, laughing with us.

It felt like someone was slowly easing a soldering iron into the side of my head. It kept going. The fire growing and growing in my brain. I grabbed at my head and fell to my knees and I looked at Derrick, his face torn with rage. He clawed at his face. Raking his fingers down over his eyes. Then he launched himself at me.

He fell on me quicker than I could react. Tearing at my clothes. The pain in my head left me weak. Too weak to fight him off as his fingers started to dig into my flesh.

He screamed but I couldn't hear the words he was making. If they were words at all. The fire raged in my head, blocking out everything around me. My vision was going. My hearing was gone. I could feel his fingers as they tore into me, taking chunks from my arm, but the pain was duller than I expected.

And he stopped.

And he looked down at me.

And he smiled.

He pulled himself off me and stood. He brushed himself off. The smile growing wider.

The pain in my head had subsided.

He was staring at the window.

He kept staring. Locked in place.

The smile growing wider. He didn't look like Derrick anymore. He looked like an animal mimicking Derrick. Some strange animal stripped to the bone.

He began to saunter to the window. A slow, steady stride. Joy in his step. Like he owned the place.

At the window he kept on walking. The window blocked his path but his stride didn't break. Just kept on walking in place.

The window started to give way around him. As though he was being sucked into the window. He looked at peace. The window wasn't breaking, it was melting as he moved through it until finally he passed through and he started his descent towards the ground 23 floors below.

Left behind was a Derrick shaped hole. As though the hole had always been there and had always been his shape.

I dared not walk over to the window for fear it would do the same to me.

The pain began anew. Sharp stabs into me. Pain that made me howl and weep and moan.

Into the black.

Into the black.

Into the black.

And I would like to tell you that none of this matters, that there was no way that any of this could matter. But it did. I could feel it inside me now.

Chapter 45

You go to the fridge. Open it. There is a smell that shouldn't be coming from it. You have to pick through food that has gone out of date. Meals that once would have brought a morsel of joy in an otherwise relentlessly bland day. Meals that someone worked on the day before, or the morning it was placed in the fridge. The power is still on.

Towards the back of the fridge, you spy the crinkled wrapper of a fast food cheeseburger. You know from sight it's a cheeseburger. They always wrap them in yellow so the fast food slaves can spot them at a glance. Fish is wrapped in blue because the ocean. Chicken is wrapped in green which isn't a colour you want to see on chicken but for some reason in all of our minds, green is chicken.

Someone put a container of nuts in the fridge. They look premium. Artisanal salted. Hand packaged. Perfect nuts picked from a pile of imperfection. Likely cost a fortune. You stop, and wonder what sort of maniac you have been working with that would refrigerate nuts.

It gives you an idea. You close the fridge after taking the cheeseburger and the nuts. You prowl the floor. Looking through people's desks. There is hardly anyone around. You curse the people that lock up their drawers before leaving for the day. They are long gone and you will never find the keys. You wonder for a moment if the facilities manager holds a master key for the desk drawers. It would take too much effort for you to find out, you never worked out where she was located, just seemed to appear on the floor sometimes, a jovial person that knew everyone and was always up for a chat.

In an area that is deserted you hit the mother load. A stash of candy. From the two dollar store, but you know that people that pay top price for candy are suckers. The best candy you can get always comes from the two dollar store. It is always the juiciest, the individual portions the biggest, the flavours the simplest and best. Candy is something we get hooked on as children so when it comes to candy, the palette never develops past childhood. The sense memory of biting into a jube is one that floods us with memories of our earliest days when the world was full of possibility and we could do anything. When an afternoon could contain endless adventures.

No one needs candy infused with the taste of cocktails on warm Central American beaches, a hint of sea salt in the mix to remind the sense of those long ago holidays. No one needs candy that tastes of apple layered with cardamon. They need jelly like blobs of matter where green tastes of lime, red tastes of strawberry in the most artificial way, and no one ever wants the black ones because no one wants licorice mixed in with their candy because that is what old people eat.

My haul in my hands, I lounge at my desk and greedily shovel the food into my maw. The nuts an excellent entree. The cheeseburger riddled with preservatives that meant it would still taste fresh months from now, the perfect main course. As dessert, easily a half kilogram of the choicest candy to end the meal in style.

And no need to hide my crime.

Chapter 46

The Work wanted me to stay in the office. If there were so few of us left then I would need to stay until The Work was done.

The television in the meeting room only showed an emergency broadcast graphic now. It had been regular programming until The Man had got up in the house of his peers some four hours ago and started ranting about the time being at hand.

His face had started to shake and hadn't stopped for a full five minutes. Like it was being shaken by unseen hands. When it stopped shaking, his face was bloodied and he looked possessed by a demon. Eyes red. Mouth foaming blood. Then he dropped to the floor. And the politicians clicked their tongues and sat, waiting for someone to tell them what to do.

What was left of the internet that wasn't the vilest of viral videos (the animals being pulled apart, the children being murdered, the screams, the screams, the screams) was virtually dedicated to showing The Man's frenzy on loop.

Every once in a while the deputy head or the head would appear on the 23rd. At first they just looked around. After a few times, they had approached, cautiously, and asked me what I was still doing. The Work. I told them I was doing The Work because someone would have to. And they would think for a moment and nod and mutter about recovery and tell me to keep up the good work and I would smile a wide smile.

I'd catch a glimpse of Charlie from time to time. He had always been good at making himself largely invisible. He wouldn't come over and talk to me. We'd never had much to say to one another during the before times.

We needed something for when this was all over. Some sort of a recovery package. Those businesses that had been in a zombie state during the crisis would need help to spin up again. It was down to me. Tax breaks. Incentives to bring business in but without displacing existing business. No one wants to come out of this facing a market failure due to excess competition.

I worked.

I worked.

When The Work would allow me to take a break, I would stand and look out the window. The fires everywhere in the city. They were beautiful.

During one break it looked like the floor was far larger than I remembered it being. I was pushing myself to the limit, tricks of the mind.

I needed to eat.

I needed to sleep.

The Work was almost done. There would be more work but it could wait. I needed the comfort of my home. The place where I could properly relax. Perhaps *Pummelled by Monkeys!* was still running. Perhaps there was a hot new show. Perhaps there would even be someone left out there that I could reach through the internet and we could talk about the hot new show until one of us succumbed.

I took a knife out of the lunch room, I would need protection out in the real world. A quick glance in the fridge but there was nothing left now.

In my apartment the TV showed only the emergency broadcast graphic.

The internet only showed The Man.

Chapter 47

I came back to the office early. The Work had been flitting in and out of my head all night. I kept being woken by the Shriek. Every time I woke, I was greeted by the cold light of the emergency broadcast system. I pulled myself off the couch in the grey light before dawn broke. My mind was on fire with ideas, policies, incentives, levers. My face gripped by an immovable smile. There was fire in my veins.

The office floor stretched out for miles. It took me most of the morning to make my way over to the windows. I considered turning on my computer and launching into The Work but first I wanted to take stock of the day and the world. I wanted to feel the pulse of the windows.

It was morning but outside it looked like midnight. Fires raged down on the street. We were on the 23rd floor but it looked like I would fall for hours before I hit the ground.

I stood and watched. I felt fire. The river still flowed. I felt fire. Birds flew in the sky but their chirps were ragged howls.

I felt the presence of Charlie on the floor.

Charlie joined me. We could be the last two left.

"I'm sorry I ended up with your job, Charlie."

"It was bound to happen one day. I just figured that retiring would be what got you the promotion. Or maybe my own promotion."

"I guess. I was thinking last night when the Shrieks kept coming. My nose started to bleed they were coming so fast at one point. Maybe the reason this didn't affect us like it did everyone else, that we didn't end up walking off into the sunset or throwing ourselves out that window, is because when we became servants we stopped being real people. We stopped existing in the real world. Like our superpower is having no interior life."

"So what are you going to do, Brian? Are you saying we're the heroes the earth needs in the face of the apocalypse? That you're going to put on a cape and go out there and fight, whatever all of this is?"

"You're a fucking idiot, Charlie. I'm not going to fight anything. How do you fight the unknowable? How do you fight God?"

"You think this is God?"

"I don't know, Charlie. I don't know. Maybe it is. It could be anything. Whatever it is, there's nothing left to do. There is nothing left outside and it's been long enough since there was anything inside."

I swear music started playing. A steady droning beat. But it didn't matter.

My head was aflame with language of all sorts. Words that I had never spoken.

Snippets of lives I had never lived.

Flames lapped at the world.

Dark hands reached to grab me from beyond.

I lived a totality of lives.

I was reduced to nothing.

Happiness flooded me.

The desks taunted me.

The computers smiled.

My phone began to talk.

From across the river, a building shouted at me, "Into the black."

I swear Charlie said, "Down the 700 steps."

And I replied, "Into the black."

Or perhaps there was nothing.

Perhaps I grinned.

Perhaps I wept.

I saw a daughter I never had.

A wife that would have comforted me.

Myself as a child weeping by the side of the road.

Ancestors and descendants that would never be.

I took the few steps to the window and kept walking. The glass didn't seem to break or push back against me. It just seemed to have a weakness that was the perfect size for me. It felt like it held me.

And I walked.

And I fell.

And the music played.

And for a moment I glimpsed the infinite.

In all it's cold, hard form.

Stretching.

Stretching.

The lesions down below laughed.

The lesions, that had snaked their way up the building, wept as I passed.

Stretching out.

And then I was on the pavement and it was dark.

There was a roar that lasted forever.